NAGUIB MAHFOUZ

KHUFU'S WISDOM

———

Naguib Mahfouz is the most prominent author of Arabic fiction today. He was born in 1911 in Cairo and began writing at the age of seventeen. His first novel was published in 1939. Since then he has written nearly forty novel-length works and hundreds of short stories. In 1988 Mr. Mahfouz was awarded the Nobel Prize in Literature. He lives in the Cairo suburb of Agouza with his wife and two daughters.

Raymond Stock (translator) is writing a biography of Naguib Mahfouz. He is the translator of Naguib Mahfouz's *Voices from the Other World* and *The Dreams*.

THE FOLLOWING TITLES BY NAGUIB MAHFOUZ ARE
ALSO PUBLISHED BY ANCHOR BOOKS:

The Beggar*
The Thief and the Dogs*
Autumn Quail*
The Beginning and the End
Wedding Song†
Respected Sir†
The Time and the Place and Other Stories
The Search†
Midaq Alley
The Journey of Ibn Fattouma
Miramar
Adrift on the Nile
The Harafish
Arabian Nights and Days
Children of the Alley
Echoes of an Autobiography
The Day the Leader Was Killed
Akhenaten, Dweller in Truth
Voices from the Other World
Rhadopis of Nubia

The Cairo Trilogy:
Palace Walk
Palace of Desire
Sugar Street

*†published as omnibus editions

KHUFU'S WISDOM

KHUFU'S WISDOM

A Novel of Ancient Egypt

———

NAGUIB MAHFOUZ

Translated from the Arabic
by Raymond Stock

ANCHOR BOOKS
A DIVISION OF RANDOM HOUSE, INC.
NEW YORK

Translator's Introduction

In September 1939, as World War II erupted in distant Europe, a Coptic, Fabian socialist magazine proprietor in Egypt named Salama Musa honored a promise he had made to a gifted writer of short stories and essays that he had frequently featured in his avant-garde journal, *al-Majalla al-jadida* ("The New Review"). Musa published twenty-seven-year-old Naguib Mahfouz's novel *'Abath al-aqdar* ("The Mockery of the Fates"), making it a special supplement, "a gift to subscribers," to that month's issue.[1]

This was not the first book-length work that Mahfouz, born in December 1911 in the old Islamic quarter of Cairo called Gamaliya, had brought to Musa, who had been his mentor for a decade. The precocious Mahfouz had started sending articles on philosophical, social science, and literary topics to Musa while still enrolled at the Fu'ad I secondary school in the modern suburb of Abbasiya, to which his family had moved from Gamaliya a few years before. Musa, a political acolyte of George Bernard Shaw, had enthusiastically accepted these erudite, well-written pieces, that always came to him by mail—then nearly went into shock when their teenaged author paid him a visit. In 1932, Musa published Mahfouz's debut book, *Misr al-qadima* ("Ancient Egypt"), a translation into Arabic of a young reader's guide to the land of the pharaohs by a British scholar of early religions, the Rev. James Baikie. Mahfouz had also done this work while still at Fu'ad I, though by the time it appeared in print he was in the midst of his studies at the Egyptian University (now Cairo University), where he earned a bachelor's degree in philosophy in 1934.

During the 1930s, Mahfouz presented several novels to Musa for his consideration. The first three failed to meet the shrewd Shavian's artistic (and/or commercial) approval. But a fourth one—set in Egypt's Old Kingdom, in the reign of the renowned Fourth Dynasty monarch, Khufu (Cheops, r. 2609–2584 B.C.), for whom the Great Pyramid of Giza was built—proved the charm. Mahfouz wove the book's plot out of an ancient Egyptian fable told in truncated form in Baikie's book, known as *Hordjedef's Tale* (from a series of stories called *Khufu and the Magicians*, preserved on the Papyrus Westcar in Berlin).[2] This work appealed to Musa's own passion for things pharaonic, inflamed by the national pride that bolstered the patriotism of his generation, that of the 1919 movement for Egyptian independence led by Sa'd Pasha Zaghlul, and the revolutionary 1922 discovery of Tutankhamun's tomb. Yet Musa did not like the title that Mahfouz had given it: *Hikmat Khufu* ("Khufu's Wisdom"). This, he told his stunned protégé, "wouldn't be popular." Instead, he suggested the catchy but unoriginal replacement, *'Abath al-aqdar* ("The Mockery of the Fates")—which has remained its title in its original language. Mahfouz found the title switch ironic. "The really peculiar thing," he later said, "is that Salama Musa had named his own son Khufu!"[3]

Whatever the new title's merits, few of the five hundred extra copies of *'Abath al-aqdar* that Musa gave Mahfouz to distribute to bookstores were sold.[4] At the time, only one brief review in a rival magazine seems to have appeared. "The story-writer Naguib Mahfouz may be young and newly arrived on the scene," wrote Muhammad Jamal al-Din Darwish in *al-Risala* on October 2, 1939, "but I put him among the most prominent members of the first rank. His stories in *al-Riwaya* [another periodical to which Mahfouz contributed] support that claim." Darwish also praised the novel's vividly descriptive prose and "easy style," and its author for making the historically remote figure of Khufu seem "as though he were actually here among us, enjoying life."[5] Even more portentous (given Mahfouz's later career as a major writer for the Egyptian screen), Darwish says that "the reader finds the chapters flowing by as though in a film strip." But beyond this welcome cheer, there was silence.

Undaunted, Mahfouz—himself obsessed with the same pharaonic nationalism that had aroused his mentor—went on to publish two more novels set in the pharaonic era, *Radubis* (*Rhadopis of Nubia*, 1943) and *Kifah Tiba* (*Thebes at War*, 1944), plus a handful of short stories with ancient Egyptian themes. Some of these (particularly *Rhadopis of Nubia*, *Thebes at War*, and such stories as "The Mummy Awakens" ("Yaqzat al-mumiya'," 1939) he used as vehicles to critique current social and political problems beneath a historical veneer. Inspired by the works of Sir Walter Scott, he had, he later said, intended to write a series of forty novels with ancient Egyptian themes. Yet though he won his first literary award for *Rhadopis of Nubia*, and received his first major recognition for *Thebes at War*, none of the three pharaonic novels was a commercial success, and most critics have tended to underrate them ever since. By 1945, Mahfouz had completely shifted to more contemporary motifs—a phase that lasted nearly forty years. Among the principal reasons: he had discovered that due to lax censorship, he could write about the present with stories set in the present, rather than beneath the cloak of the past.

Naguib Mahfouz became the most acclaimed Arab novelist with his legendary *Cairo Trilogy* (*Palace Walk*, *Palace of Desire*, and *Sugar Street*, set mainly in his own childhood haunts of Gamaliya and Abbasiya between the World Wars), for which he won Egypt's State Prize in 1957. Two years later, militant Islamist shaykhs led crowds in protests against his next novel, *Awlad haratina* (*Children of the Alley*), an allegory of humankind's rise and confrontation with tyranny from the era of Adam and Eve to the age of modern science, as it was being serialized in the Cairene daily, *al-Ahram*. As a result, this novel was banned from publication as a book in Egypt. (In October 1994, for having failed to repent for this novel, Mahfouz was stabbed in the neck by a religious fanatic. The assault nearly killed him, and for more than four years robbed him of the ability to write.) While he made his living as a civil servant, first in the Ministry of Religious Endowments, then in the Ministry of Culture (until retiring in 1971), he nonetheless has produced nearly sixty books of fiction—the majority set in twentieth-century Cairo. During his more than seven decades as a writer, he has moved from strict realism to various forms of allegory, in works that are increasingly concise and abstract. That would certainly describe the one- to three-paragraph serial micronovellas that he is now producing under the title *Ahlam fatrat al-naqaha* ("Dreams of Recovery"), which wreck the criticism by some of later generations that he is hoarily passé. Even in old age, he has remained ahead of the creative curve of most of his allegedly more au courant younger rivals—as he likewise had, all his life, over the majority of his own contemporaries.

The simultaneous publication of English translations of Mahfouz's early pharaonic triad of novels for his ninety-second birthday nearly completes the correction of a historical oversight—the neglect (especially in this language) of this writer's fiction with ancient Egyptian themes. The American University in Cairo Press began this process in 1998 by bringing out his 1985 novel, *al-'A'ish fi-l-haqiqa*, as *Akhenaten: Dweller in Truth*. Next came *Voices from the Other*

World: Ancient Egyptian Tales, a collection of short stories, in 2002. Only one final known work from this genre remains, his 1983 novel-in-dialogue, *Amama al-'arsh* ("Before the Throne"), in which many of the nation's rulers, from Mina (founder of the First Dynasty) to Anwar al-Sadat, are brought before the Osiris Court, which ancient Egyptians believed judged the souls of the dead.

While Mahfouz read a great deal of Egyptology to research these works, he also prized literary effect over period accuracy. To cite examples from *Khufu's Wisdom*: Egyptians did not use horses or even wheeled vehicles until nearly a thousand years after the time frame of this story. Nor is there evidence that artists of that day hired studios or hung out signs to advertise their creations, or made miniature portraits that could be concealed in one's clothes. Much affected by Hellenic philosophy as well as the accounts of Herodotus and Strabo, Mahfouz marked the landscape with Greek place names—some of which are Egyptianized here—and even adapted Plato's concept of the philosopher-king to the case of Khufu. And, though he preserved the element of the fabulous from the ancient tale that inspired his own, he wanted his readers to identify as much as possible with the lives of his characters—who, despite the obvious inconsistencies, operate in an environment rich in a semblance of real ancient Egyptian beliefs, places, and institutions. In the end, he truly does, as his lone reviewer noted in 1939, make Khufu (and his retinue) seem to come alive.

Mahfouz's works as a whole are likely to give him a kind of immortality invented—though in a very different form—by the ancient Egyptians. William Kelly Simpson quotes from a text in the Papyrus Chester Beatty IV (translated by A. H. Gardner): "A man has perished, and his corpse has become dust. . . . But writings cause him to be remembered in the mouth of the story teller."[6] Most often, the person commemorated, however, was not the actual author. When the earliest literary works appeared, during the Middle and New Kingdoms, if the writer was mentioned, this was often either a real or apocryphal figure who lived a millennium or more before. For example, in *Khufu's Wisdom*, the sage Kagemni cited by various characters was an actual vizier of the Sixth Dynasty, but putatively placed in the Fourth—though the only manuscript of his famous *Teaching* (supposedly written to him, not by him) dates to the Twelfth Dynasty.[7] (Given the strong moral in Mahfouz's novel, it was partly this sort of "instruction" or "wisdom" writing—to which the original title slyly refers—that inspired the work itself. The same is true for most of Mahfouz's pharaonica.)

Hence, true authorial renown would have been unexperienced in the days of Khufu, Tutankhamun, or even the mighty Ramesses II. Of the great figures among the pharaohs, only Akhenaten—claimed to be the first monotheist to rule a state—has survived the millennia through his ideas. But Mahfouz has not sought to found a new faith, only to reaffirm an old one—mainly, in the beauty and durability of the written word. His own words would endure even without his Nobel Prize in Literature, awarded in 1988—the first such recognition for a writer in Arabic.

The translator wishes to thank Roger Allen, Kathleen Anderson, Hazem Azmy, Brooke Comer, Humphrey Davies, Gaballa Ali Gaballa, Zahi Hawass, Salima Ikram, Shirley Johnston, Klaus Peter Kuhlmann, Khofo Salama Moussa, Raouf Salama Moussa, Richard B. Parkinson, Donald Malcolm Reid, Rainer Stadelmann, Helen Stock, Peter Theroux, Patrick Werr, and David Wilmsen for their helpful comments on the present work, as well as Kelly Zaug and R. Neil Hewison, again for their sensitive editing. And, once more, he is most grateful to Naguib Mahfouz, for kindly answering so many queries about this material.

This translation is dedicated to the author, and to M.S.V.L.

1 Telephone interview with Khofo Salama Moussa, September 19, 2003.
2 For a translation, see Richard B. Parkinson, *The Tale of Sinuhe and Other Ancient Egyptian Poems, 1940–1640 B.C.* (Oxford: Clarendon Press, 1997), pp. 102–127.
3 Interview with Naguib Mahfouz, June 4, 2000.
4 Interview with Raouf Salama Moussa, June 19, 2003.
5 Muhammad Jamal al-Din Darwish, *al-Risala* (Cairo), October 2, 1939, pp. 1921–1922. See also 'Ali Shalash, *Najib Mahfuz: al-tariq wa-l-sada* (Beirut: Dar al-Adab, 1990), pp. 108–109 and 151.
6 William Kelly Simpson, ed., *The Literature of the Ancient Egyptians: An Anthology of Stories, Instructions, and Poetry* (New Haven and London: Yale University Press, 1972), p. 1.
7 Parkinson, *The Tale of Sinuhe*, pp. 246 and 290–292.

KHUFU'S WISDOM

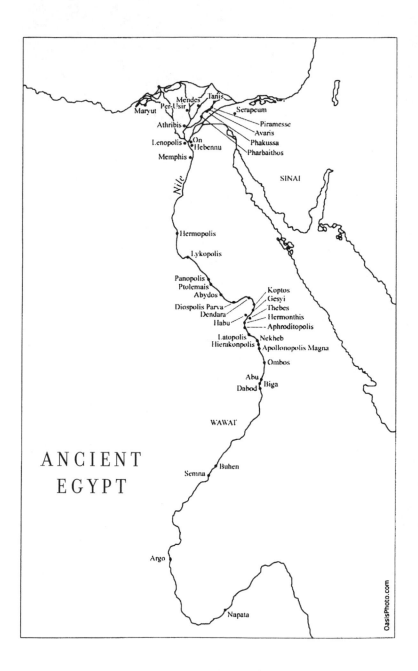

Maryut
Mendes
Per-Usir
Tanis
Serapeum
Athribis
Piramesse
Avaris
Lenopolis
On
Phakussa
Hebennu
Pharbaithos
Memphis

SINAI

Nile

Hermopolis

Lykopolis

Panopolis
Ptolemais
Koptos
Abydos
Gesyi
Diospolis Parva
Thebes
Dendara
Hermonthis
Habu
Aphroditopolis
Latopolis
Nekheb
Hierakonpolis
Apollonopolis Magna
Ombos

Abu
Dabod
Biga

WAWAT

ANCIENT
EGYPT

Buhen
Semna

Argo

Napata

1

The Possessor of Divine Grandeur and Lordly Awe, Khufu, son of Khnum, reclined on his gilded couch, on the balcony of the antechamber overlooking his lush and far-flung palace garden. This paradise was immortal Memphis herself, the City of the White Walls. Around him was a band of his sons and his closest friends. His silken cloak with its golden trim glistened in the rays of the sun, which had begun its journey to the western horizon. He sat calmly and serenely, his back resting on cushions stuffed with ostrich feathers, his elbow embedded in a pillow whose silk cover was striped with gold. The mark of his majesty showed in his lofty brow and elevated gaze, while his overwhelming power was displayed by his broad chest, bulging forearms, and his proud, aquiline nose. He bore all the dignity of his two-score years, and the glorious aura of Pharaoh.

His piercing eyes ran back and forth between his sons and his companions, before shifting leisurely forward, where the sun was setting behind the tops of the date palms. Or they would turn toward the right, where they beheld in the distance that eternal plateau whose eastern side fell under the watchful gaze of the Great Sphinx, and in whose center reposed the mortal remains of his forebears. The plateau's surface was covered with hundreds and thousands of human forms. They were leveling its sand dunes and splitting up its rocks, digging out the mighty base for Pharaoh's pyramid—

which he wanted to make a wonder in the eyes of human-kind that would endure for all the ages.

Pharaoh cherished these family gatherings, which refreshed him from his weighty official duties, and lifted from his back the burden of habitual obligations. In them he became a companionable father and affectionate friend, as he and those closest to him took refuge in gossip and casual conversation. They discussed subjects both trivial and important, trading humorous stories, settling sundry affairs, and determining people's destinies.

On that distant day, long enclosed in the folds of time—that the gods have decreed to be the start of our tale—the talk began with the subject of the pyramid that Khufu wanted to make his eternal abode, the resting place for his flesh and bones. Mirabu, the ingenious architect who had heaped the greatest honors on Egypt through his dazzling artistry, was explaining this stupendous project to his lord the king. He expounded at length on the vast dimensions desired for this timeless enterprise, whose planning and construction he oversaw. Listening for a while to his friend, Pharaoh remembered that ten years had passed since the start of this undertaking. Not hiding his irritation, he reminded the revered craftsman, "Aye, dear Mirabu, I do believe in your immense ingenuity. Yet how long will you keep me waiting? You never tire of telling me of this pyramid's awesomeness. Still, we have yet to see one layer of it actually built—though an entire decade has passed since I marshaled great masses of strong men to assist you, assembling for your benefit the finest technical resources of my great people. And for all of that, I have not seen a single trace on the face of the earth of the pyramid you promised me. To me it seems these mastaba tombs in which their owners still lie—and which cost them not a hundredth of what we have spent so far—are mocking the great effort we have expended, ridiculing as mere child's play our colossal project."

Apprehension rumpled Mirabu's dusky brown face, wrinkles of embarrassment etching themselves across his broad brow. With his smooth, high-pitched voice, he replied, "My lord! May the gods forbid that I ever spend time wantonly or waste good work on a mere distraction. Indeed, I was fated to take up this responsibility. I have borne it faithfully since making it my covenant to create Pharaoh's perpetual place of burial—and to make it such a masterpiece that people will never forget the fabulous and miraculous things found in Egypt. We have not thrown these ten years away in play. Instead, during that time, we have accomplished things that giants and devils could not have done. Out of the bedrock we have hewn a watercourse that connects the Nile to the plateau upon which we are building the pyramid. Out of the mountains we have sheared towering blocks of stone, each one the size of a hillock, and made them like the most pliable putty, transporting them from the farthest south and north of the country. Look, my lord—behold the ships: how they travel up and down the river carrying the most enormous rocks, as though there were tall mountains moving along it, propelled by the spells of a monstrous magician. And look at the men all absorbed in their work: see how they proceed so slowly over the ground of the plateau, as though it were opening to reveal those it has embraced for thousands of years gone by!"

The king smiled ironically. "How amazing!" he said. "We commanded you to build a pyramid—and you have dug for us a river, instead! Do you think of your lord and master as a sovereign of fish?"

Pharaoh laughed, and so did his companions—all but Prince Khafra, the heir apparent. He took the matter very seriously. Despite his youth, he was a stern tyrant, intensely cruel, who had inherited his father's sense of authority, but not his graciousness or amiability.

"The truth is that I am astounded by all those years that

you have spent on simply preparing the site," he berated the architect, "for I have learned that the sacred pyramid erected by King Sneferu took much less time than the eons you have wasted till now."

Mirabu clasped his hand to his forehead, then answered with dejected courtesy, "Herein, Your Royal Highness, dwells an amazing mind, tireless in its turnings, ever leaning toward perfection. It is the fashioner of the ideal, and—after monumental effort—a gigantic imagination was created for me whose workings I expend my very soul in bringing to physical reality. So please be patient, Your Majesty, and bear with me also, Your Royal Highness!"

There was a moment of silence. Suddenly the air was filled with the music of the Great House Guards, which preceded the troops as they retired to their barracks from the place where they had been standing watch. Pharaoh was thinking about what Mirabu had said, and—as the sounds of the music melted away—he looked at his vizier Hemiunu, high priest of the temple of Ptah, supreme god of Memphis. He asked with the sublime smile that never left his lips, "Is patience among a king's qualities, Hemiunu?"

Tugging at his beard, the man answered quietly, "My lord, our immortal philosopher Kagemni, vizier to King Huni, says that patience is man's refuge in times of despair, and his armor against misfortunes."

"That is what says Kagemni, vizier to King Huni," said Pharaoh, chuckling. "But I want to know what Hemiunu, vizier to King Khufu, has to say."

The formidable minister's cogitation was obvious as he prepared his riposte. But Prince Khafra was not one to ponder too cautiously before he spoke. With all the passion of a twenty-year-old born to royal privilege, he declared, "My lord, patience is a virtue, as the sage Kagemni has said. But it is a virtue unbecoming of kings. Patience allows ministers and obedient subjects to bear great tribulations—but the greatness of kings is in overcoming calamities, not enduring them. For this reason, the gods have compensated them for their want of patience with an abundance of power."

Pharaoh tensed in his seat, his eyes glinting with an obscure luminescence that—were it not for the smile drawn upon his lips—would have meant the end for Mirabu. He sat for a while recalling his past, regarding it in the light of this particular trait. Then he spoke with an ardent fervor that, despite his forty years, was like that of a youth of twenty.

"How beautiful is your speech, my son—how happy it makes me!" he said. "Truly, power is a virtue not only for kings, but for all people, if only they knew it. Once I was but a little prince ruling over a single province—then I was made King of Kings of Egypt. And what brought me from being a prince into possession of the throne and of kingship was nothing but power. The covetous, the rebellious, and the resentful never ceased searching for domains to wrest away from me, nor in preparing to dispatch me to my fate. And what cut out their tongues, and what chopped off their hands, and what took their wind away from them was nothing but power. Once the Nubians snapped the stick of obedience when ignorance, rebellion, and impudence put foolish ideas into their heads. And what cracked their bravura to compel their submission, if not power? And what raised me up to my divine status? And what made my word the law of the land, and what taught me the wisdom of the gods, and made it a sacred duty to obey me? Was it not power that did all this?"

The artist Mirabu hastened to interrupt, as though completing the king's thought, "And divinity, my lord."

Pharaoh shook his head scornfully. "And what is divinity, Mirabu?" he asked. "'Tis nothing if not power."

But the architect said, in a trusting, confident tone, "And mercy and affection, sire."

Pointing at the architect, the king replied, "This is how

you artists are! You tame the intractable stones—and yet your hearts are more pliant than the morning breeze. But rather than argue with you, I'd like to throw you a question whose answer will end our meeting today. Mirabu, for ten years you have been mingling with those armies of muscular laborers. By now you must truly have penetrated their innermost secrets and learned what they talk about among themselves. So what do you think makes them obey me and withstand the terrors of this arduous work? Tell me the honest truth, Mirabu."

The architect paused to consider for a moment, summoning his memories. All eyes were fixed upon him with extreme interest. Then, with deliberate slowness, speaking in his natural manner—which was filled with passion and self-possession—he answered, "The workers, my lord, are divided into two camps. The first of these consists of the prisoners of war and the foreign settlers. These know not what they are about: they go and they come without any higher feelings, just as the bull pushes around the water wheel without reflection. If it weren't for the harshness of the rod and the vigilance of our soldiers, we would have no effect on them.

"As for those workers who are in fact Egyptians, most of them are from the southern part of the country. These are people with self-respect, pride, steadfastness, and faith. They are able to bear terrific torment, and to patiently tolerate overwhelming tragedies. Unlike those aliens, they are aware of what they are doing. They believe in their hearts that the hard labor to which they devote their lives is a splendid religious obligation, a duty to the deity to whom they pray, and a form of obedience owed to the title of him who sits upon the throne. Their affliction—for them—is adoration, their agony, rapture. Their huge sacrifices are a sign of their subservience to the will of the divine man that imposes itself over time everlasting. My lord, do you not see them in the blazing heat of noon, under the burning rays of the sun, striking at the rocks with arms like thunderbolts, and with a determination like the Fates themselves, as they sing their rhythmic songs, and chant their poems?"

The listeners were delighted, their blood gladdened in a swoon of gaiety and glory, and contentment glowed on Pharaoh's strong, manly features. As he rose from his couch, his movement sent all those in attendance to their feet. In measured steps, he processed with dignity down the broad balcony until he reached its southern edge. Contemplating its magnificent view, he peered into the remote expanse at that deathless plateau of the dead on whose holy terrain were traced the long lines of toilers. What augustness, and what grandeur! And what suffering and struggle in their pursuit! Was it right for so many worthy souls to be expended for the sake of his personal exaltation? Was it proper for him to rule over so noble a people, who had only one goal—his own happiness?

This inner whispering was the only disturbance that beat from time to time in that breast filled with courage and belief. To him it appeared like a bit of wandering cloud in heavens of pure blue, and, when it came, it would torment him: his chest would tighten, his very serenity and bliss would seem loathsome to him. The pain worsened, so he gave the pyramids plateau his back—then wheeled angrily upon his friends, catching them off guard. He put to them this question: "Who should give up their life for the benefit of the other: the people for Pharaoh, or Pharaoh for the people?"

They were all struck speechless, until the commander, Arbu, broke through them excitedly, calling out in his stentorian voice, "All of us together—people, commanders, and priests—would give our lives for Pharaoh!"

Prince Horsadef, one of the king's sons, said with intense passion, "And the princes, too!"

The king smiled vaguely, the anxiety easing on his sublime face, as his vizier Hemiunu said, "My lord, Your Divine Majesty! Why differentiate your lofty self from the people of Egypt, as one would the head from the heart or the soul from the body? You are, my lord, the token of their honor, the mark of their eminence, the citadel of their strength, and the inspiration for their power. You have endowed them with life, glory, might, and happiness. In their affection there is neither humiliation nor enslavement; but rather, a beautiful loyalty and venerable love for you, and for the homeland."

The king beamed with satisfaction, returning with long strides to his golden divan. As he sat down, so did the rest. But Prince Khafra, the heir apparent, was still not relieved of his father's earlier misgivings.

"Why do you disturb your peace of mind with these baseless doubts?" he said. "You rule according to the wish of the gods, not by the will of men. It is up to you to govern the people as you desire, not to ask yourself what you should do when they ask you!"

"O Prince, no matter how other kings may exalt themselves—your father need only say, 'I am Pharaoh of Egypt,'" Khufu rejoined.

He then seemed to swell up as he said with a booming voice—yet as though speaking to himself, "Khafra's speech would be appropriate if it were directed toward a weak ruler—but not toward Khufu, the omnipotent—Khufu, Pharaoh of Egypt. And what is Egypt but a great work that would not have been undertaken if not for the sacrifices of individuals? And of what value is the life of an individual? It equals not a single dry tear to one who looks to the far future and the grand plan. For this I would be cruel without any qualms. I would strike with an iron hand, and drive hundreds of thousands through hardships—not from stupidity of character or despotic egotism. Rather, it's as if my eyes were able to pierce the veil of the horizons to glimpse the glory of this awaited homeland. More than once, the

queen has accused me of harshness and oppression. No—
for what is Khufu but a wise man of far-seeing vision, wear-
ing the skin of the preying panther, while in his breast there
beats the heart of an openhanded angel?"

A long silence settled upon them, his companions longing
for their nightly session of exquisite small talk, so they might
forget their ponderous troubles. All of them hoped that the
king, after he'd had his fill of projects and purposes, would
propose some entertaining sport, or invite them to a party
with libations and song. But in those days Khufu complained in his leisure hours of boredom with the palace and
its spectacular aspects. When he learned that the time for
diversion had come, he would grow weary, looking around
at his friends as though in a daze. Hence, Hemiunu queried,
"Has my lord filled his cup with drink?"

Pharaoh nodded his head. "I drank today, as I drank yesterday."

"Shall we call in the lady musicians, sire?"

Indifferently, he answered, "I listen to their music night
and day."

Mirabu interjected, "What would my lord think about
going on a hunt?"

The king responded in the same tone, "I'm fed up with
the chase, be it on land or water."

"In that case, what about strolling among the trees and
flowers?"

"Is there, in this valley, a beautiful sight that I have yet to
behold?"

The king's laments saddened his loyal retainers—all except Prince Hordjedef, who was saving a delicious surprise
for his father, of which Pharaoh had no hint.

"O my father the king," said Hordjedef, "I am able to
bring right before you, if you desire, an amazing magician who
knows the secrets of life and death, and who is able merely
to command something to be, and it is."

Khufu said nothing, this time not hastening to reaffirm his boredom. He looked at his son with interest, for the king followed closely the news of the wizards and their wonders, enjoying what was said about their rare contrivances. Pleased that he would be seeing one of them before him, he asked his son, "Who is this magician, Prince Hordjedef?"

"He is the sorcerer Djedi, my lord. He is a hundred and ten years old, but still strong as a young tough. He has an astonishing power to control the will of both man and beast, and vision that can penetrate the Veil of the Invisible."

Pharaoh grew intrigued, his ennui waning. "Can you bring him to me here, now?" he said.

"Please bear with me a few moments, sire!" the prince replied, joyfully.

Hordjedef stood up and saluted his father with a prolonged bow—then rushed off to fetch the fabulous magician.

2

Soon Prince Hordjedef returned with a tall, broad-shouldered man walking before him. The man's gaze was sharp and piercing. His head was crowned with a mane of soft white hair, and a long, thick beard fell over his breast. Wrapped in a loose robe, he steadied his step with a crude, massive cane.

The prince bowed low and announced, "My lord! I present your obedient servant, Djedi the magician."

The sorcerer prostrated himself before the king, kissing the ground between his feet. Then he said, in a powerful voice that made all those who heard it quake: "My lord, Son of Khnum, Radiance of the Rising Sun and Ruler of the Worlds, long live his glory, and may happiness settle within him forever!"

Pharaoh eyed the wizard warmly and sat down close to him, saying, "How have I not seen you before, when you have preceded me into the light of this world by all of seventy years?"

The superannuated sorcerer answered in a kindly tone, "May the Lord grant you life, health, and strength: the likes of me are not favored to appear before you without being asked."

Regarding him benignly, the king pressed him, "Is it true that you can make miracles, Djedi? Is it true that you can force your will on both man and beast, and that you can snatch the Veil of the Invisible from the face of Time?"

The man nodded his head until his beard bounced on his chest. "That verily is true, sire," he replied.

"I would like to see some of these miracles, Djedi," answered Pharaoh.

And so came the frightful hour. The eyes of those watching widened, their faces full of obvious fascination. Djedi did not rush to his task, but stood frozen for a long while as though turned into stone. Then he shot a sharp-toothed grin as he looked them over quickly.

"To my right there beats a heart that does not believe in me," said Djedi.

Those gathered were shocked, and exchanged confused glances. The monarch was pleased with the keen eye of the magician, and turned to ask his men, "Is there one among you who denies the truth of Djedi's miracles?"

Commander Arbu shrugged his shoulders disdainfully, then marched before the king. "My lord, I do not believe in magic tricks. I see them as a kind of sleight of hand, a skill for those who have the time to devote to it," he said.

"What's the point of talking when we have the man right before us?" said Khufu. "Go bring him a lion and turn it loose upon him. We'll see how he tames it with his magic and bends it to his will."

But the commander was not satisfied. "Please forgive me, sire," he said, "but I have no dealings with lions. However, as I'm standing right in front of him, perhaps he could try his magical art on me. If he so wishes—that is, to make me believe in him—then he could force me to submit to his will, and wrench control of my own strength from me."

A heavy silence fell. The faces of some of those assembled seemed anxious, while others expressed exultation or the simple love of gawking. Both groups looked at the magician to see what he would do with the obstinate commander.

They huddled about him as he stood quietly and serenely, a confident smile stuck to his thin, angular lips. Pharaoh let out a huge laugh, asking in a voice not lacking in sarcasm, "Arbu, do you really hold yourself so little dear?"

With stunning self-assurance, the commander replied, "My self, sire, is strong, thanks to the strength of my mind—which mocks the conceits of mere legerdemain."

At this, anger flashed on the face of Prince Hordjedef. Aiming his vehement speech directly at the commander, he said to the king, "Let what you wish come to pass. If it pleases my lord, may Djedi be permitted to respond to this challenge?"

Pharaoh gazed upon his furious son, then told the wizard, "Very well, then—let us see how your sorcery overcomes the might of our friend Arbu."

Commander Arbu stood regarding the magician with an arrogant glare. He wanted to turn his face away from him with contempt—then felt a power pulling at him from within the man's eyes. Seething with rage, he struggled to turn his neck, to wrench loose his gaze from the over-whelming attraction that held it fast. Instead, weak and frustrated, he found his eyes locked into the bulging, gleam-ing orbs of Djedi, which burned and blazed like a pair of crystals reflecting the rays of the sun. Their brilliance out-shone that in Arbu's own eyes, which darkened as the light of the world seemed to fade out of them. The great soldier's strength disappeared with it, as he sank into submission.

When Djedi was convinced that his preternatural power had taken full effect, he stood up tall and erect. Pointing to his seat, he shouted at the commander imperiously, "Sit down!"

Arbu carried out the order slavishly. He staggered like a drunk, throwing himself onto the chair with an air of doomed compliance, in a state of total devastation.

A disbelieving "Ah!" escaped the lips of those present.

Prince Hordjedef smiled with relief and pride. As for Djedi, he looked respectfully at Khufu, saying with an easy grace, "Sire, I am able to make him do whatever is desired, and he would be powerless to resist a single demand. Yet I am reluctant to do this to a man such as he, one of our homeland's most estimable commanders, and of Pharaoh's personal companions. So I ask, is my lord satisfied with what he has seen?"

Khufu nodded his head as though to say, "Yes."

Quickly going over to the bewildered commander, the sorcerer ran his nimble fingers over Arbu's brow, reciting in a faint voice a peculiar incantation. Little by little the man began to revive, the life gradually creeping back into his senses until his consciousness returned. For a while he remained like a person perplexed, peering all around him as though knowing nothing of what he saw. Then his eyes rested on Djedi's face—and he remembered. His cheeks and his forehead flushing a deep red, he avoided looking at the fearsome fellow as he rose from his seat, stumbling embarrassed and vanquished along the balcony's floor.

The king smiled at him, upbraiding him gently, "How falsehood had possessed you!"

The commander bowed his head and mumbled, "Lofty is the power of the gods—their wonders are exalted on earth and in heaven!"

To the magician, the king then remarked, "You have done well, O most able man. But have you the kind of authority over the Unseen that you have over the minds of created beings?"

"I do indeed, my lord," Djedi replied confidently.

Khufu fell deep into thought, contemplating what sort of questions to ask the magician. At length his face brightened with the light of revelation. "Can you tell me," he inquired, "if one of my seed is destined to sit on the throne of Egypt's kings?"

The man seemed gripped with fear and unease. Pharaoh perceived what troubled him.

"I grant you full freedom to speak," he said. "I assure you there will be no penalty for whatever you say."

Djedi glanced meaningfully at the face of his lord—then tilted his head toward the sky, absorbed in fervent prayer. He continued this, without moving or speaking, for a full hour. When he returned to confront the king, his kin, and the courtiers, his skin had turned sallow, his lips white, and his countenance confused. The group grew alarmed as they sensed the approach of imminent evil.

His patience exhausted, Prince Khafra demanded, "What's wrong with you that you don't speak, when Pharaoh has guaranteed your immunity from harm?"

The man choked down his panting breath as he addressed the king, "Sire, after you, no one from your seed shall sit upon the throne of Egypt."

His speech was a blow to those gathered, like a sudden gale in the branches of a tranquil tree. They stared at him viciously with eyes so furious that the whites seemed to fly out of them. Pharaoh's brow furrowed: he glowered like a lion driven mad with rage. Prince Khafra's face turned pale as he pursed his cruel lips, his expression broadcasting his anguish and loss.

As if to soften the impact of his prophecy, the sorcerer added, "You shall rule safely and securely, my lord, until the end of your long and happy life."

Pharaoh shrugged his shoulders dismissively, then said with a frightful voice, "He who labors for his own sake labors in vain. So stop trying to console me and simply tell me: do you know whom the gods have reserved to succeed them on the throne of Egypt?"

"Yes, I do," said the wizard. "He is an infant newly born, who had not seen the light of the world until this very morning."

"Who are his parents, then?"

"His father is Monra, high priest of the Temple of Ra at On," answered Djedi. "As for his mother, she is the young Ruddjedet, whom the priest married in his old age so that she would bear him this child—which the Fates have written shall be a ruler of Egypt."

Khufu rose combatively, like a great cat aroused. Standing with the full stature of Pharaoh, he took two steps toward the sorcerer. Suppressing a gasp, the man averted his gaze, as the king asked him, "Are you utterly sure of what you are saying, Djedi?"

"All that the page of the Unseen has disclosed to me, I have revealed to you," the magician replied, hoarsely.

"Fear not, nor be distressed," said the king. "You have delivered your prophecy, and now you shall reap the bounty it has earned for you."

Summoning one of the palace chamberlains, Pharaoh ordered him to treat Djedi the magician hospitably, and to give him fifty pieces of gold as a reward. The man then accompanied Djedi as they both left the scene.

Prince Khafra was sorely stricken—his eyes bursting with the remorselessness in his heart, his steely face like a harbinger of death. As for his father, Khufu, he did not waste his outrage in a fit of shouting and wild gesticulations. Rather, he held it in check with the force of his inner will, transforming it into a daring resolve that could level great mountains and make the cosmic powers stir.

He turned to his vizier, asking him grandly, "What do you think, Hemiunu: does it avail to be warned against Fate?"

The vizier raised his eyebrows in thought, but nothing issued from his lips, white with panic and dismay.

"I see that you are afraid to say the truth, and are considering disavowing your own wisdom in order to please me," said the king, scoldingly. "But no, Hemiunu, your lord is too great to be upset by being told the truth."

Though not a flatterer, Hemiunu was a coward. Nonetheless, he was sincerely loyal to the king and the crown prince, and took pity on their pain. When the two appeared as though they would not be angry at what he might say, he replied, almost inaudibly, "My lord! I am in accord with the words of wisdom that the gods imparted to our forebears, and to their propagator, Kagemni, on the question of Destiny—which hold that precaution cannot thwart Fate."

Khufu looked at his heir apparent and asked, "And what, O Prince, is your view of this matter?"

The prince looked back at his father with eyes blazing like a beast caught in a trap.

Pharaoh smiled as he declaimed, "If Fate really was as people say, then creation itself would be absurd. The wisdom of life would be negated, the nobility of man would be debased. Diligence and the mere appearance of it would be the same; so would labor and laziness, wakefulness and sleep, strength and weakness, rebellion and obedience. No, Fate is a false belief to which the strong are not fashioned to submit."

The zeal fired in his breast, Commander Arbu shouted, "Sublime is your wisdom, my lord!"

Pharaoh, still smiling, said with absolute composure, "Before us is a suckling child, only an easy distance away. Come then, Commander Arbu—prepare a group of chariots, which I will lead to On—so that I myself may look upon this tiny offspring of the Fates."

"Will Pharaoh himself be going?" Hemiunu asked, amazed.

"If I don't go now to defend my own throne," said Pharaoh, laughing, "then when will it be right for me to do so? Very well, now—I invite you all to ride with me to witness the tremendous battle between Khufu and the Fates."

3

Pharaoh's squadron of one hundred war chariots streamed out of the palace, manned by two hundred of the toughest troopers of the Great House Guards. Khufu—amidst a cohort of the princes and his companions—took their lead, with Khafra at his right and Arbu on his left.

They sped away to the northeast, shaking the ground of the valley like an earthquake, along the right branch of the Nile, heading toward the city of On. Their wheels rattling like thunder, the rushing vehicles, with their magnificently adorned horses, kicked up mountains of dust behind them that hid them from the eyes of beautiful Memphis. With the colossal men riding them—like statues bedecked with swords, bows, and arrows, and armored with shields—they reminded the sleeping earth of the soldiers of Mina. They too had thrown up their own dust on these same roads hundreds of years before, bearing to the North an undeniable victory, forging the nation's unity as their glorious legacy.

They rolled onward over the stones and gravel, led by an all-powerful man, the very mention of whose name humbled hearts and caused eyes to be lowered. Yet they rode not to invade a nation or to combat an army. Rather, to besiege a nursing baby boy still in his swaddling clothes, blinking his eyes at the light of the world—launched by the words of a wizard that threatened the mightiest throne on earth, shaking the stoutest hearts in creation.

They covered the floor of the valley with surpassing speed, circumventing villages and hamlets like a fleeting arrow, fixing their eyes onto that fearsome horizon that loomed over the suckling child whom the Fates had made to play such a perilous role.

From afar there appeared to them a cloud of dust whose source their eyes couldn't make out, until, the distance slowly dwindling, they were able to discern a little band of horsemen crossing in their direction. They had no doubt that this group came from the district of Ra.

The horsemen drew closer, and it became clear that they were mounted soldiers trailing behind a single rider. The nearer they approached, the clearer it seemed they were pursuing that rider. Then, as the king's squadron came right upon their goal, they gasped with disbelief—for at their lead was a woman seated bareback on a stallion. The plaits of her hair had come undone, and were strewn about behind her by the wind, like pennants on the head of a sail, and she looked exhausted. Meanwhile, the others had caught up with her from behind, surrounding her on every side.

This happened just as the king arrived with his retinue. The royal chariot had to slow down to avoid a collision, though neither Pharaoh nor any of his men paid much heed to either the woman being pursued, or her pursuers. They presumed these were policemen carrying out some official-duty or other, and would have passed them by without any contact but for the woman calling out to them, "Help me, O Soldiers—Help me! Those men won't let me reach Pharaoh. . . ."

Pharaoh's chariot halted, and so did those behind him. He looked at the men encircling the woman and called to them with his commanding voice, "Summon her to me."

Yet, ignorant of he who had made this command, they did not respond. One of the horsemen's officers came forward, saying roughly, "We are guards from On who have come to execute an order from its high priest. From what city are you, and what do you want?"

The officer's folly enraged Pharaoh's troopers. Arbu was about to berate him, but Pharaoh flashed him a hidden sign. Seething, he remained silent. The invocation of the Ra priest's name had diverted Pharaoh from his anger and made him think. Hoping to draw the officer into conversation, Khufu asked him, "Why were you pursuing this woman?"

Self-importantly, the officer replied, "I am not obliged to account for my mission except to my chief."

Pharaoh shouted with thunderous fury, "Release this woman!"

The soldiers were now certain that they were dealing with a formidable figure. They gave up on the object of their chase, who had scurried to the king's chariot, cowering beneath it fearfully, calling out all the while, "Help me sir, please help me!"

Arbu clambered down from his chariot and marched forcefully up to the officer. When the officer saw the sign of the eagle and Pharaoh's emblem on Arbu's shoulder, terror defeated him. Sheathing his sword, he stood to attention and gave a military salute, calling out to his men, "Hail the commander of Pharaoh's guards!"

They all returned their swords to their scabbards, and stood in file like statues.

When the woman heard what the officer said, she realized that she was in the presence of the Great House Guards. Standing up before Arbu, she said, "Sir, are you truly the head of our lord the king's guards? Naught but the truth of the gods is guiding me to him . . . for I fled my mistress, sir, in order to go to Pharaoh's palace, to the king's doorstep— for love of whom the lips of every Egyptian, man or woman, would gladly kiss."

"Do you have some wish to be fulfilled?" Arbu asked her.

The woman replied, panting, "Yes, sir. I harbor a menacing secret that I wish to disclose to the Living God."

Pharaoh listened more intently, as Arbu asked her, "And what is this menacing secret, my good woman?"

"I will divulge it to the Holy Eminence," she said, entreatingly.

"I am his faithful servant, discreet with his secrets," Arbu assured her.

The woman hesitated, glancing anxiously at those present. Her color was pale, her eyes darted back and forth, and her heart was pounding hard. The commander saw that he could entice her to speak by being soft with her.

"What is your name," he inquired, "and where do you live?"

"My name is Sarga, sir. Until this morning I was a servant in the palace of the high priest of Ra."

"Why were they chasing you?" Arbu continued. "Had your master made an accusation against you?"

"I'm an honorable woman, sir, but my master abused me."

"Did you then flee because of his mistreatment?" Arbu pressed on. "Are you requesting that your complaint be raised with Pharaoh?"

"No, sir—the matter is much more threatening than you think. I stumbled upon a secret of whose danger I must warn Pharaoh—so I fled to warn the Sacred Self, as duty compels me. My master dispatched these soldiers in my wake, to come between me and my sacred trust!"

The officer's horsemen trembled, as he quickly said in their defense, "The Reverend One ordered us to arrest this woman as she fled on horseback on the road to Memphis. We carried out the order without knowing anything at all about why it was given."

Then Arbu said to Sarga, "Are you going to accuse the high priest of Ra of treason?"

"Summon me to Pharaoh's threshold so that I may reveal to him what so oppresses me."

His patience expiring, Pharaoh fretted at the loss of precious time.

"Was the priest blessed this morning with the birth of a son?" he asked the woman, abruptly.

She turned toward him, wobbling with wonder. "Who informed you of this, sir," she blurted, "when they had kept it secret? This is truly amazing!"

Pharaoh's entourage was becoming curious, exchanging silent looks among themselves. Meanwhile, the king interrogated her in his awe-instilling voice, "Is this the secret that you want Pharaoh to know?"

The woman nodded, still confused, "Yes, it is, sir—but it's not all that I wish to tell him."

Pharaoh spoke sharply, in an intensely commanding tone that brooked no delay, "What is there to say, then? Tell me."

"My mistress, Lady Ruddjedet, began to feel labor pains at dawn," Sarga burst out, fearfully. "I was one of the chambermaids stationed by her bed to relieve her discomfort—sometimes with conversation, otherwise with medicine. Before long, the high priest entered; he blessed our mistress and prayed fervently to Our Lord Ra. As though wishing to put our mistress at ease, he gave her the glad tidings that she would give birth to a baby boy. This boy, he said, would inherit the unshakeable throne of Egypt, and rule over the Valley of the Nile as the successor to the God Ra-Atum on earth.

"He said to her, hardly able to contain himself for joy—as though he had forgotten my presence: I—whom she trusted more than any other servant—that the statue of the god Ra had told him this news in his celestial voice. But when his gaze fell upon me, his heart beat loud enough to be heard, and the fear was clear on his face. In order to appease the evil whisperer within, he had me arrested and held in the grain shed. Yet I was able to escape, to mount a steed, and set out upon the road to Memphis to tell the king what I had learned. Evidently, my master sensed that I had fled—for he sent these soldiers to apprehend me that, if not for you, would have carried me back to my death."

Pharaoh and his companions listened to Sarga's story with alarmed surprise—for it confirmed the prophecy of Djedi the magician. Prince Khafra was gravely worried. "Let not the warning we received have been in vain!" he barked.

"Yes, my son—we shouldn't waste time."

Khufu turned to the woman. "Pharaoh shall reward you very well for your fidelity," he said. "There's nothing else for you to do now but to tell us which way you would like to go."

"I wish, sir, that I might go safely to the village of Quna where my father lives."

"You are responsible for her life until she reaches her home," Pharaoh said to the officer, who nodded his head in obedience.

Motioning to Commander Arbu, the king climbed back onto his chariot, ordering his driver to proceed. They took off like the Fates themselves, with the other chariots behind them, in the direction of On, whose surrounding wall and the heads of the pillars of its great sanctuary, the Temple of Ra-Atum, could already be seen.

4

At that moment the high priest of Ra was kneeling at his wife's bedside in passionate prayer:

"Ra, Our Lord Creator, Present from the Time of Nothingness, from the time when the water poured into the vastness of the primeval ocean, over which weighed a heavy darkness. You created, O Lord, by Your power, a sublimely beautiful universe. You filled it with an enchanting orderliness, easing its unified rule over the spinning stars in the heavens, and over the abundant grain on the earth. You made from the water all living things: the birds soaring in the sky, the fish swimming in the sea, man roaming on the land, the date palm flourishing in the parching desert. You have spread through the darkness a radiant light, in which Your majestic face is revealed, and which spreads warmth and life itself to all things. O Lord Creator, I confide to You my worry and my sorrow; I beseech You to lift from me the anguish and the tribulation, for I am Your faithful servant and Your believing slave. O God, I am weak—so grant me strength from Your cosmic knowledge; O God, I am fearful—so grant me confidence and peace. O God, I am threatened by a great evil—so enfold me in Your vigilance and Your compassion. O God, in my old age, You have endowed me with a son; You have blessed him and written for him, in the annals of the Fates, that he shall be a ruling king—so keep all malice away from him, and repel the evil that is set against him."

Monra recited this prayer with an unsteady voice. His eyes flowed with hot tears that trickled down his thin and drawn cheeks. They wet his hoary beard, as he raised up his aged head, looking with emotion upon the pallid face of his wife, confined to her childbed. Then he gazed upon the tiny infant, serenely raising the lids from his little dark eyes, which he had lowered in fear of the strange world around him. When his wife Ruddjedet sensed that Monra had ceased his praying, she said to him weakly, "Is there any news of Sarga?"

"The soldiers will catch up with her," the man sighed, "if the Lord so commands."

"Alas, my lord! The thread of our child's life hangs on something so uncertain?"

"How can you say that, Ruddjedet? Since Sarga escaped, I have not stopped thinking of a way to protect the two of you from evil. The Lord has guided me to a ruse, yet I fear for you, because in your delicate condition you might not be able to bear any hardships."

She stretched out a hand toward him imploringly. "Do what you can to save our child," she said in a pleading tone. "Let not my frailty worry you, for maternity has given me a strength that healthy people do not possess."

"You should know, Ruddjedet," the tormented priest replied, "that I have prepared a wagon and filled it with wheat. In it I have readied a corner for you to lie with our son. I have fashioned a box made of wood so that if you lay yourselves within it you will be concealed from view. In this you will go with your handmaiden Kata to your uncle in the village of Senka."

"Call the servant Zaya, because Kata's in childbed—just like her mistress," said Ruddjedet. "She delivered a baby boy of her own this morning."

"Kata has given birth?" Monra replied, taken aback. "In any case, Zaya is no less loyal than Kata."

"And what about you, my husband?" said Ruddjedet. "What if Fate decides that the secret of our child should reach Pharaoh, and he sends his soldiers to you. How will you answer when they ask you about your son and his mother?"

The high priest had not prepared any plan to save himself if what she warned of occurred. Distracted as he was by the need to save both mother and child, he had given it little thought. Hence he lied when he answered, "Don't worry, Ruddjedet. Sarga will not get away from those I have sent after her. Whatever happens, no crisis will catch me unawares—and my news will reach you very soon."

Fearing any increase in her anxiety, he wanted to distract her, so he stood up and called out loudly for Zaya. The servant came rapidly and bowed to him in respect.

"I shall entrust to you your mistress and her newborn child," Monra told her, "so that you may conduct them to the village of Senka. You must take care, and be wary of the danger that threatens them both."

"I would sacrifice myself for my mistress," she answered, sincerely, "and for her blessed son."

The priest asked her to assist him in carrying her mistress to the grain shed. Surprised by his request, the servant nonetheless obeyed his command. The man wrapped his wife with a soft quilt, and put his hand under her head and shoulders, while Zaya lifted her from under her back and thighs. Together they walked with her to the outer hallway, descending the staircase to the courtyard. They then entered the shed, laying her on the spot that he had prepared for her in the wagon. This done, the priest went back up and returned with his son, who sobbed and cried. He kissed him lovingly, and placed him in the embrace of his mother. He watched them for a little while from the side of the wagon.

When he saw Ruddjedet becoming upset, he said to her, his heart skipping a beat, "Calm yourself for the sake of our dear child, and don't allow fear a way into your heart."

"You haven't named him yet," she said, weeping.

Smiling, he replied, "I hereby name him with the name of my father, who reposes next to Osiris. *Djedef . . . Djedefra . . . Djedef son of Monra*. By God, I shall make his name blessed, and defend him from the wiles of those who plot against him."

The man approached with the wooden box and placed it over the pair so dear to him. Zaya sat in the driver's seat, taking the reins of the two oxen, as Monra told her, "Go with the blessings of the Lord our keeper."

As the wagon began to move slowly on its way, his eyes filled with copious tears, through which he watched as the vehicle crossed the courtyard, until the gate blocked his view. He dashed to the staircase, climbing it with the vigor of a young man, then hurried to the window that looked out upon the road, observing the wagon as it carried his heart and his joy beyond his sight.

Something surprising then occurred that he had thought never would—certainly not with the speed that it now did. As he looked on, he was seized with an inexpressible terror. He forgot the sorrow of their parting, the agony of their farewell, and his longing as a father. The fear became so inflamed that he lost all sense and perception: he clenched his fists, pounding his breast with them, as he mumbled in dismay, "O Lord Ra, O Lord Ra." He kept repeating this unconsciously as his eyes saw the squadron of royal chariots suddenly appear on the bend in the road near the temple. They drew closer and closer to his palace, precisely arrayed in assault formation, with equally precise and orderly speed, exactly two paces between each chariot.

"O Lord of Heaven, Pharaoh's soldiers have come more quickly than the mind could conceive. Their arrival trumpets the success of Sarga's mission, and her escape from my soldiers. If only You had been able to send the angels of sudden death as speedily!" he thought.

Pharaoh's troops drew near like giant demons, their horses neighing, their wheels rumbling, their helmets gleaming in the slanting rays of the sun. And why had they come? They came to slay the innocent child, the beloved son, with whom the Lord had gladdened him in his age of despair.

Monra was still beating his breast with his fists, shaking his head like an imbecile, wailing in lament for his son. "O Lord . . . a group of them are surrounding the wagon; one of them is questioning poor Zaya sternly. What is he asking her? How does she answer him? And what do they seek? The lives of both my child and my wife depend on a single word uttered by Zaya. O My God! O Sacred Ra! Make her strong and secure, place on her tongue the words of life—and not of death! Save Your beloved son to live out the Fate that You have decreed for him, which You have proclaimed to me."

Hours seemed to be passing slowly as the soldier continued questioning Zaya, stopping her departure. O God—what if one of them should move the box or just peer into it, wondering what was inside? What if the child should cry, or moan, or wail?

"Be still, my son. . . . By the Lord, if only your mother would place her nipple in your mouth. Should a sigh escape you now, it would be like a sentence of death. . . . My Lord, my heart is breaking, my soul is ascending into heaven. . . ."

Suddenly, the priest fell silent. His eyes widened and he gasped—but this time, from overwhelming joy. *"Praise be to Ra!"* he wept. "They are letting the wagon go safely on its way: in the name of Ra is her flight and her refuge. Praise be to You, O Merciful Lord."

5

The priest breathed a deep sigh of relief and felt—from happiness—a longing to weep. He would have done so if he had not remembered what hardships and terrors still awaited him. His feeling of security lasted but a few brief moments. He paced slowly over to a table and picked up a silver pitcher, pouring out enough of its clear water to quench his burning thirst. Soon, however, his ears rang with the shrill sound of the powerful force that had arrived in his palace courtyard—and whose mission was to kill the newborn that had just come within a mere two bow lengths, or nearer, to the danger of death.

Driven by fear, a servant approached him, telling him that a detachment of the king's guards had occupied the palace and was watching its exit. Then another servant came, saying that the head of the force had sent an order demanding that he come to them quickly. Making a show of being calm and collected, Monra spread his sacred cloak over his shoulders and placed his priestly headdress on his head. Then he left his chamber with deliberate steps, displaying the true dignity and majesty of On's great religious personage. The priest did not slight his own prestige, but stopped, facing the courtyard at the doorstep of the reception hall, casting a superficial glance at the soldiers of the force standing motionless in their places, as if they were statues from a previous age. Then he lifted his hand in greeting and said in his cultured voice, without looking at anyone in particular, "You are all most welcome. May the Divine Ra, Shaper of the Universe and Creator of Life, bless you."

He heard an awesome voice answer him, "Any thanks owed are to you, O Priest of Sacred Ra."

His body jumped at the sound of the voice, like a lamb at the roar of a lion. His eyes searched for its owner until they settled on the force's center. When he realized that Pharaoh himself had come to his home, he was terrified and astonished. He did not hesitate to do what was obliged, but hastened to his doorway, avoiding nothing. When Pharaoh's chariot pulled up to him, he prostrated himself before it.

"My lord Pharaoh, Son of the Lord Khnum, Light of the Rising Sun, Giver of Life and Strength," he called out, quaveringly. "I, my lord, implore the God that He may inspire your great heart to overlook my neglect and my ignorance, and to obtain your pardon and satisfaction."

"I pardon the errors of honest men," the king told him.

His heart fluttering, Monra inquired, "Why does my lord grace me with a visit to my humble palace? Please come and assume its guidance."

Pharaoh smiled as he descended from his chariot, following Prince Khafra and his brother princes, along with Hemiunu, Arbu, and Mirabu. The priest proceeded onward, with the king following him, succeeded in turn by the princes and his companions, until they stopped in the reception hall. Khufu sat in the center with his retinue around him. Monra tried to excuse himself to prepare the obligatory hospitality, but Pharaoh said instead, "We absolve you of your duties as host—we have come on a very urgent mission: there is no time for dallying."

The man bowed. "I am at my lord's beck and call," he said.

Khufu settled into his seat, and asked the priest in his penetrating, fear-inspiring voice, "You are one of the elite men of the kingdom, advanced in both knowledge and in wisdom. Therefore can you tell me: why do the gods enthrone the pharaohs over Egypt?"

The man answered with the assurance of faith, "They select them from among their sons, endowing them with their divine spirit to make the nation prosper, and the worshippers glad."

"Well done, priest—for every Egyptian strives for his own welfare and that of his family," said the king. "As for Pharaoh, he bears the burden for the masses, and entreats the Lord on their behalf. Thus, can you tell me what Pharaoh must do regarding his throne?"

With transcendent courage, Monra replied, "What is incumbent upon Pharaoh to do regarding his throne is what the faithful man must do with the charge entrusted to him by the generous gods. That is, he must carry out his obligations, claim his proper rights, and defend that which he must with his honor."

"Well done again, virtuous priest!" Khufu said, nodding his head in satisfaction. "So now inform me, what should Pharaoh do if someone threatens his throne?"

The brave priest's heart pounded. He was certain that his answer would determine his fate. Yet, as a pious and dignified man of religion, he was determined to tell the truth.

"His Majesty must destroy those with ambitions against him."

Pharaoh smiled. Prince Khafra's eyes glinted grimly.

"Excellent, excellent . . . because if he does not do so, he would betray his custodianship from the Lord, forget his divine trust, and forfeit the rights of the believers."

The king's face grew harsher, showing a resolution that could shake even mountains. "Hear me, priest—he who poses a threat to the throne has been exposed."

Monra lowered his eyes and held his tongue.

"The Fates are making mock as is their wont," Khufu continued, "and have conjured a male child."

"A male child, sire?" the priest ventured, quaking.

Anger sparked in Pharaoh's eyes. "How, priest, can you be so ignorant?" he shouted. "You have spoken so keenly of honesty and credibility—so why do you let a lie slink into your heart right before your master? You surely know what we do—that you are this child's father, as well as his prophet!"

The blood drained from the priest's face, as he said in surrender, "My son is but a suckling child, only a few hours old."

"Yet he is an instrument in the hands of the Fates—who care not if their tool is an infant or an adult."

A calm silence spread suddenly among them, while a frightful horror reigned over all as they held their breath, awaiting the word that would let fly the arrow of death at the unfortunate child. Prince Khafra's forbearance failed him, his brows creasing, his naturally severe face growing even harder.

"O Priest," the king intoned, "a moment ago you declared that Pharaoh must eliminate whoever threatens his throne—is this not so?"

"Yes, sire," the priest answered, in despair.

"No doubt the gods were cruel to you in creating this child," said Khufu, "but the cruelty inflicted on you is lighter than that which has been inflicted on Egypt and her throne."

"That is true, my lord," Monra murmured.

"Then carry out your duty, priest!"

Monra fell speechless; all words failed him.

"We—the community of Egypt's kings—have an inherited tradition of respect and caring for the priesthood," Pharaoh continued. "Do not force me to break it."

How amazing! What does Pharaoh mean by this? Does he want the priest to understand that he respects him and would not like to slay his son—and that therefore, it is necessary that he undertake this mission, from which the king himself recoils? And how can he ask him to kill his own child by his own hand?

Truly, the loyalty that he owed to Pharaoh obliged him to execute his divine will without the least hesitation. He knew for certain that any individual from among the Egyptian people would gladly give up his soul in order to please great Pharaoh. Must he then take his own dear son and plunge a dagger into his heart?

Yet who had decreed that his son should succeed Khufu on the throne of Egypt? Was it not the Lord Ra? And hadn't the king declared his intention to kill the innocent child, in defiance of the Lord Creator's will? Who then must he obey—Khufu or Ra? And what would Pharaoh and his minions do, who are waiting for him to speak? They're becoming restless and angry—so what should he do?

A dangerous thought came to him rapidly amidst the clamor of confused embarrassment, like a flash of lightning among dark clouds. He remembered Kata, and her son—to whom she had given birth that very morning. He recalled that she was sleeping in the room opposite that of her mistress. Truly, this was a fiendish idea of which a priest like himself ought to be totally innocent, but any conscience would yield if subjected to the pressures that now assailed Monra before the king and his men. No—he was unable to hesitate.

The cleric bowed his heavy head in respect, then went off to carry out a most abominable crime. Pharaoh followed him; the princes and the notables trailing behind. They mounted to the highest floor behind him—but when they saw the high priest begin to enter the room's door, they stopped, silent, in the hallway. Monra, wavering, turned toward his lord.

"Sire, I have no weapon with which to kill," he said. "I possess not even a dagger."

Khufu, staring, did not stir. Khafra felt his chest tighten. He withdrew his dagger, shoving it brusquely into the high priest's hand.

Trembling, the man took it and hid it in his cloak. He entered the chamber, his feet almost unable to bear his weight. His arrival awoke Kata, who smiled at him gratefully, believing that her master had come to give her his blessings. She revealed the face of the blameless child, telling him wanly, "Thank the Lord with your little heart, for he has made up for the death of your father with divine compassion."

Horrified and panicked, Monra's spirit abandoned him: he turned away in revulsion. His emotions overflowing, their torrent swept away the froth of sin. But where could he find sanctuary? And how would it all end? Pharaoh was standing at the door—and there wasn't a moment to pause and reflect. His confusion grew more and more profound, until his mind was dazed. He bellowed in bewilderment, then— drawing a deep breath—he unsheathed his dagger in a hopeless gesture, thrusting its blade deep into his own heart. His body shuddered dreadfully—then tumbled, stiff and lifeless, to the floor.

Enraged, the king entered the room, his men in train. They all kept peering at the high priest's corpse, and the terrified woman in childbed, her eyes like glass. All, that is, except Prince Khafra, whom nothing would deflect from his purpose. Worried that the golden opportunity would be wasted, he drew his sword and raised it dramatically in the air. He brought it down upon the infant—but the mother, swift as lightning, instinctively threw herself over her son. Yet she was unable to frustrate the Fates: in one great stroke, the saber severed her head—along with that of her child.

The father looked at his son, and the son looked at his father. Only the vizier Hemiunu could rescue them from the anxious silence that then overcame them. "May it please my lord," he said, "we should leave this bloody place."

They all went out together, without speaking.

The vizier suggested that they leave for Memphis immediately, so they might reach it before nightfall. But the king disagreed.

"I will not flee like a criminal," he said. "Instead, I will summon the priests of Ra, to tell them the story of the Fates that sealed the calamitous ruin of their unfortunate chief. I shall not return to Memphis before that is done."

6

The wagon ambled on behind two plodding oxen, with Zaya at the reins. For an hour it paced down On's main thoroughfare, before pulling away from the city's eastern gate. There it turned toward the desert trail that led to the village of Senka, where Monra's in-laws lived.

Zaya could not forget the frightful moment when the soldiers surrounded her, interrogating her as they looked closely at her face. Yet she felt—proudly—that she had kept her wits about her, despite the terror of her position, and that her steadiness had persuaded them to let her go in peace. If only they knew what was hidden in the wagon!

She remembered that they were tough soldiers indeed. Nor could she forget what enlivened the magnificence of the man who approached them. She would never forget his awesome manner, or his majestic bearing, which made him seem the living idol of some god. But, how incredible—that this stately person had come to kill the innocent infant who had only seen the light of the world that very morning!

Zaya glanced behind her to see her mistress, but found her wrapped under the quilt, as his lordship the high priest had left her. "What a wretched woman—no one could imagine such an atrocious sleep for a lady who had just given birth," the servant thought. "Her great husband did not dream of such hardships as those the Fates had sent to her. If he could have known the future, he would not have wished to be a father—nor would he have married Lady Ruddjedet, who was twenty years his junior!"

Yet, miserable, she moaned to herself, "If only the Lord would grant me a baby boy—even if he brings me all the troubles in the world!"

Zaya was an infertile wife aching for a child that she wished the gods would give her, like a blind person hoping for a glimpse of light. How many times had she consulted physicians and sorcerers? How many times had she resorted to herbs and medicines without benefit or hope? She shared the despair of her husband, Karda, who suffered the most intense agony to see life going on year after year without the gift of a child to love in his home, to warm him with the promise of immortality. He bid her farewell for the last time as he prepared to depart for Memphis, where he worked in building the pyramid—threatening to take a new wife if she failed to produce a child. He had been gone for one month, two months, ten months—while she had monitored herself for the signs of pregnancy hour by hour, to no avail. O Lord! What was the wisdom of making her a woman, then? What is a woman without motherhood? A woman without children is like wine without the power to intoxicate, like a rose without scent, or like worship without strong faith behind it.

Just then she heard a faint voice calling, "Zaya." She rushed to the wooden box, lifting it up and opening its side, and saw her mistress along with her child, whom she held in her arms. Worn out from exertion, Ruddjedet's lovely brown face had lost its color, as Zaya asked her, "How is your ladyship?"

"I am well, Zaya, thank the gods," she answered weakly. "But what about the danger that threatens us now?"

"Be reassured, my mistress," the servant replied. "The peril to you and my little master is now far away."

The lady sighed deeply. "Do we still have a long trip ahead?" she asked.

"We have an hour, at the very least, left before us," Zaya said amiably. "But first you must sleep in the Lord Ra's protection."

The lady sighed again and turned to the slumbering infant, her pale but captivating face filled with maternal love. Zaya kept looking at her and at her son, at their beautiful, joyful image, despite the pains and perils that they faced.

What a gorgeous sight they make! If only she could, just once, taste motherhood, she would gladly give her life for it! O God! The Lord shows no compassion, nor does pleading help, nor will Karda forgive her failure. Perhaps before long she will become a mere divorcée, expelled from her home, wracked by solitude and the misfortunes of being unmarried.

Zaya shifted her gaze from the happy mother to the two oxen. "If only I had a son like that!" she said to herself. "What if I take this child and pretend that he is my own, after yearning that the gods would favor me with one by natural means?"

Her intention was not evil, rather, she was being wishful—as the soul wishes for the impossible—and as it wishes for what it would not do—from fear, or compassion.

Zaya wished away, while the heavens created happiness for her under the wings of dreams. In them she saw herself walking with the exquisite child up to Karda, saying, "I have borne you this gorgeous boy." She saw her husband grin and jump for joy, kissing and hugging her and little Djedef together. Drunk from this imaginary ecstasy, she lay down on her right side, holding the two oxen's reins with one hand, while cradling her head with the other. She let her mind wander until she abandoned herself to the world of dreams, her eyes quickly numbed by the delicate fingers of sleep, veiled from the light of wakefulness, as the western horizon veils the light of the sun from the world.

When Zaya returned to the sensate world, she thought that she was greeting the morning in her bed in the palace of her benefactor, the priest of Ra. She stretched out her hand to pull the blanket around her, because she suddenly felt a cold breeze. Her hand dug into something that resembled sand. Amazed, she opened her eyes to see the cosmos blackened and the sky studded with stars. Her body felt a strange shaking—and she remembered the wagon, her mistress Ruddjedet with her little, fugitive child, and all the memories that the conquering power of sleep had snatched away from her.

But where was she? What time of night was it?

She looked around to see an ocean of darkness on three sides. On the fourth, she saw a feeble light coming from very far away, which undoubtedly emanated from the villages spread out along the bank of the Nile. Beyond that, there was no sign of life in the direction toward which the oxen were plodding.

The desolation of the world penetrated her soul, its gloom piercing her heart. A terrifying tremor made her teeth chatter with fear, while she kept peering into the darkness with eyes that expected horrors in unsettling forms.

On the dark horizon Zaya imagined that she could make out the ghostly shapes of a Bedouin caravan. She recalled what people said about the tribes of Sinai—their assaults on villages, their kidnapping of people who had wandered off the road or taken the wrong course, their interception of other caravans. No doubt the wagon that she piloted so aimlessly would be precious booty to them—with all the wheat it carried, and the oxen that hauled it. Not to mention the two women—over whom the chief of the tribe would have every right to drool. Her fear rose to the point of madness, so she stepped down onto the desert sands. As she did so, she looked at the sleeping woman and child, regarding their faces by the light of the pulsing stars. Without thought or plan, she reached out her hand and, lifting the boy up delicately, expertly wrapped the quilt around him, and set off in the direction of the city's lights. As she walked on, she thought that she heard a voice calling out to her in terror, and she believed that the Bedouin had surrounded her mistress. Her fear grew even stronger and she doubled her pace. Nothing would hinder her progress: not the heaping dunes of sand, nor the dear burden she carried, nor her enormous tiredness. She was like someone falling into an abyss, pulled down by their own weight, unable to stop their descent. Perhaps she had not gone too far into the desert, or perhaps she had covered more distance toward her goal than she could tell, because, beneath her feet, she felt hard-packed ground like the surface of the great Desert Road. Looking behind her, Zaya saw only blackness. By this time she had used up her hysterical strength: her speed slowed and her steps grew heavier. Then she fell down onto her knees, panting fearsomely. She was still insanely afraid, but couldn't move, like the victim pursued by a specter in a nightmare, but who cannot flee. She continued swiveling to her right and to her left, not knowing in which direction could come escape—or ruin.

Suddenly, she fancied that she could hear the rumble of chariots and the whinnying of horses! Did she really see wheels and vehicles, knights and steeds—or was it just the blood throbbing in her ears and her brain? But the voices became clearer, until she was certain that she could make out the forms of the riders returning from the north. She did not know if they came in peace—or to kill her. Nor was it possible to hide, because Djedef had begun to sob and cry. Not feeling safe from the plunging chariots while kneeling in the center of the road, she shouted, "Charioteers! Look here!"

She called out to them again—then surrendered herself to the Fates. The chariots drew up quickly, then stopped a short distance away. She heard a voice ask who was shouting—and she thought it was not unfamiliar. She gripped the child more firmly as though to warn him, and putting on an uncouth, countrified accent, told them, "I'm just a woman who's gotten lost—this hard road and the scary things in the dark have worn me out. And this is my baby boy—the wind and the damp night have nearly killed him."

"Where are you going?" the owner of the first voice asked her.

"I'm heading for Memphis, sir," Zaya answered, beginning to feel assured that she was talking to Egyptian soldiers.

The man laughed and said in astonishment, "To Memphis, ma'am? Don't you know that a man mounted on a horse takes two hours to travel that far?"

"I've been walking since the midafternoon," Zaya said, plainly suffering. "Lack of means forced me to move, and I was fooled into thinking that I could reach Memphis before nightfall."

"Whom do you have in Memphis?"

"My husband, Karda. He's helping to build the Lord Pharaoh's pyramid."

The man questioning her leaned toward another in the chariot to his left, whispering a few words in his ear.

"Granted—that one soldier will escort her to her home district," the second man said.

But the first one rejoined, "No, Hemiunu—she'll find nothing there but hunger and shame. Why don't we take her to Memphis, instead?"

Obeying Pharaoh's order, Hemiunu came down from his chariot and went over to the woman, helping her to rise. He then walked to the nearest chariot and put her and her child inside it, advising the soldier within it about them.

At that moment, Khufu turned to the architect Mirabu. "Watching the massacre of that innocent mother and child, who bore neither guilt nor offence, has torn your tender heart, Mirabu," he said. "Take care not to accuse your lord of cruelty. Look at how it gratifies me to carry along a famished woman and her nursing baby to spare them the ills of hunger and cold, and deliver them to a place that they could reach by themselves only with tremendous strain. Pharaoh is compassionate to his servants. And he was not less compassionate when that ill-starred infant's fate was decreed. In this way, the acts of kings are like those of the gods—cloaked in the robe of villainy, yet, in their essence, they are actually celestial wisdom.

"The first thing you must do, O Architect Mirabu," said Prince Khafra, "is to marvel at the power of the overwhelming will that has defeated the Fates—and blotted the sentence of Destiny."

Hemiunu returned to his chariot, ordering the driver to proceed. The squadron again took off in the direction of Memphis, slicing their way through the waves of darkness.

7

Zaya arrived in Memphis just before midnight, after a short ride with the pharaonic guards. The king gave her two pieces of gold, so she sat before him thankfully—as one obliged by a debt—thinking him to be an important commander, but no more. She bid him farewell in the pitch-dark night, without seeing his face—or he seeing hers.

Zaya was in a terrible state—both in her mind, and in her body. She craved a room in which she could retire by herself, so she asked a policeman if he knew of a modest inn where she could spend the rest of the night. Finally, when she found herself and the child alone, she heaved a deep sigh of relief and threw herself down on the bed.

At last she felt released from the agony of physical pain and internal fear. Yet the terrors of her soul overshadowed the torments of her body. Drained and frightened, all that Zaya's mind's eye could see was her mistress who had just given birth, whose infant she had abducted as she abandoned her in that derelict wagon in the midst of the desert. The darkness had engulfed Ruddjedet, desolation surrounding her—while the men of pillage and plunder, who know neither mercy nor compassion—had set upon her.

Now perhaps she was a prisoner in their hands, treated only with brutality, forced into bondage and slavery. Meanwhile, she would be telling the gods of her humiliation, complaining of how she'd suffered from despair, treachery, and torture.

More and more wracked with discomfort and fear, Zaya kept tossing and turning on her bed, first right, then left, as grimacing ghosts pursued her. Begging for sleep to rescue her, she tossed and turned ever more before slumber finally lifted her from the hellfire of damnation.

She awoke to the baby's crying. The sun's rays broke through the room's tiny window, carpeting the floor with light. She took pity on the child, rocking him gently and kissing him. Sleep had alleviated her sickness and calmed her soul, though it had not rid her of worry, or her mind of torment. Yet the infant was able to divert her feelings toward him, saving her from the agony and afflictions of the night. She tried caressing him, but he sobbed even more as she confronted the problem of feeding him—which utterly perplexed her. Then she hit upon the only solution: she went to the room's door and knocked on it with her hand. An old woman came, inquiring what she wanted. Zaya asked the woman to bring her half a rotl of goat's milk.

Carrying Djedef in her arms, she walked with him back and forth across the room, putting her breast into his mouth to soothe and amuse him. She gazed at his beautiful face and sighed with a sudden thrill that seemed to have slipped unnoticed into her heart: *"Smile, Djedef—smile, and be happy—you will see your father soon."*

But no sooner had she sighed in relief than she said to herself fearfully, "Do you see how I won him despite everything? The issue of his true mother is finished—and of his true father, as well!"

As for his mother, the Bedouin had taken her prisoner, and she—Zaya—could do nothing to rescue her. If she had lingered another moment before fleeing, she too would have found herself but cold plunder in the hands of the barbarous nomads. There was no justice in taking the blame for a crime that she did not commit, so she felt no embarrassment. As regards Djedef's father, no doubt Pharaoh's soldiers killed him in revenge for helping his wife and son escape.

Thinking about these things reassured her. She went back over all of them again to appease her conscience, to put paid to the ghosts of dread and the harbingers of pain.

She told herself incessantly that she had done the most virtuous thing by kidnapping the child and running away, for if she had stayed at her mistress's side, she would not have been able to protect her against the assault—and would have perished with her, as well. After all, it was not within her ability to carry her or to give her shelter. Nor would there have been any mercy in leaving the child in Ruddjedet's arms until the men of Sinai killed him. She felt it was more of a good deed to flee, and to take Djedef with her!

However torturous these thoughts, how lovely it was to wind up with Djedef by herself, not having to share him with anyone! She was his mother without any rival, and Karda was his father. As if she wanted to be confident of this fact she kept cooing to him, saying: "Djedefra son of Karda . . . Djedefra son of Zaya."

The old woman came with the goat's milk. The make-believe mother began to nurse the infant in an unnatural manner until she thought that he had had his fill. Then there was nothing left for her but to get ready to go out to see Karda. She bathed herself, combed her hair, and put her veil over her shoulders, before leaving the inn with Djedef in her arms.

The streets of Memphis were crowded, as they usually were, with people both walking and riding—men and women, citizens, settlers, and foreigners. Zaya did not know the road to the Sacred Plateau, so she asked a constable which way to go. The plateau, he said, was "northwest of the Wall of Memphis—it would take two hours or more to get there on foot—a half hour on horseback." In her hand she clutched the pieces of gold, so she hired a wagon with two horses, seating herself in it with serenity and bliss.

No sooner had her dreams pulled her out of the world and taken her to the heaven of rapture and delight, than her imagination raced ahead of the wagon to her dear husband, Karda. With his tawny skin and brawny arms, nothing was more becoming than the effect of his short loincloth, which revealed his thighs of iron. And what was more loveable than his long face with its narrow forehead, his great nose, and widely-spaced eyes, and his broad, powerful voice with its saucy Theban drawl? How many times had she yearned to grab his forearms, kiss his mouth, and listen to him speak! In earlier reunions of this kind, when she had been gone for a long time, he had kissed her passionately and said to her caressingly, "Come now, wife—for me you are like stony ground that soaks up water, but grows nothing." This time, though, he wouldn't say it—how could he, when she meets him holding the most beautiful creature ever conceived by woman? There is nothing wrong if he stares at her in confusion, the muscles softening on his hardened face, the look in his flashing eyes dissolving into gentleness. Or as he shouts out to her, unable to contain himself for joy, "Finally, Zaya—you have born a child! Is this truly my son? Come to me—come to me!" Holding her head high in haughtiness and pride, she would say to him: "Take your child, Karda— kiss his little feet, and kneel down in thanks to the Lord Ra. He is a boy, and I have named him Djedef." She vowed to take her husband to his birthplace of Thebes, because she was still afraid—though she did not know just why exactly— of the North and its people. In lovely Thebes, under the protection of the Lord Amon, she would raise her son and love her husband, and live the life that she had been denied for so long.

She was jolted from her reverie by the clamor and chaos of Memphis. She looked ahead to see the wagon ascending the winding road, the man urging the horses onward with his whip. From her seat she could not make out the surface of the plateau, but the lively voices, clanging tools, and chants of the workers rang in her ears. Among the chants, she recognized one that Karda would sing to her in happy times:

We are the men of the South, whom the waters of the Nile
Have brought to this land, that the gods have chosen for
*   our home,*
Home of the Pharaohs—where we make the black earth
*   flourish.*
Behold the towering cities, and the temples with many
*   pillars!*
Before us, there were but ruins that sheltered beasts and
*   crows.*
For us, stone is soft and obedient, and so are the mighty
*   waters.*
Ask of our strength among the tribes of Nubia and Sinai!
Ask about our labors afar—while our chaste wives wait
*   alone.*

She listened to the men as they repeated these verses with strength and affection combined, and she longed to be with them, as the dove longs for the cooing of its mate. Her heart sang with them.

Crossing the road called the Valley of Death, the wagon arrived at the plateau. Zaya got out and walked toward the mass of men spread over the sprawling terrain like an enormous army milling about a square. On her way, she passed the Temple of Osiris, the Great Sphinx, and the mastaba tombs of the ancestors whose worldly works earned their repose within this purified ground. She saw the long channel that the workers had cut for waters from the Nile to reach the plateau. Huge boats were plying her waters, filled with massive rocks and stones, awaited by crowds of laborers with wagons crawling at the dockside. From a distance she saw the base of the pyramid that the limits of vision could not wholly take in, and the men scattered like stars on its surface. The sounds of the chanting blended with the shouts of the overseers, as well as those of the commanders of the Heavenly Guard, and the crackle of tools. Confused, Zaya stopped with the child in her arms, turning this way and that without knowing which direction to choose, and saw the futility of calling out over this depthless ocean of humanity. Her anxious, exhausted eyes rambled back and forth among all the faces.

One of the guards who passed her—thinking there was something strange about her—approached and asked her roughly, "What did you come to do here, madam?"

In all simplicity, she replied, "I'm looking for my husband, Karda, sir."

"Karda? Is he an architect or a member of the guard?" the soldier asked her, knitting his brow as he tried to remember.

"He's a laborer, sir," she said, timidly.

The man laughed sarcastically and said, pointing to a nearby building, "You can ask about him at the Inspector's Office."

Zaya walked toward her goal, an elegant building of modest size, where a military guard stood by the door, blocking her way inside. But when she told him why she had come, he made way for her. She entered a wide room, its sides lined with desks, behind which sat the employees. The walls were filled with shelves stacked with papyrus scrolls. Within the room there was a door standing ajar, toward which the guard directed her with his staff. She passed through it to a smaller chamber, more beautiful and more expensively furnished than the other. In one corner, behind an enormous desk, there was a fat, squat man, distinguished by his outsized head, short, broad nose, full face, jutting jaw, and cheeks inflated like two small water skins. His eyes bulged under heavy lids as he sat with immense conceit, inflicting his supercilious bossiness upon whoever came to him.

He sensed someone had entered—yet did not raise his eyes nor display any sign of interest until he finished what he had before him. Then he peered at Zaya with bold disdain, asking in an overbearing, vainglorious voice, "What do you want, woman?"

Embarrassed and afraid, Zaya answered weakly, "I have come to look for my husband, sir."

Again in the same tone, he asked her, "And who is your husband?"

"A laborer, sir."

He struck his desk with his fist, then said fiercely, his voice ringing out as though in a vault, "And what reason could there be for taking him from his work, and putting us to this trouble?"

Zaya grew more frightened. Confused, she did not even try to respond. The inspector continued to look at her. He noticed her round, bronze-colored face, her warm, honey-hued eyes, and her succulent youth. Hard it was for him to lay the weight of fear over a face as lovely as hers. His conspicuous power was only for show and vanity—his heart was good, his feelings refined. Taking pity on the woman, he said to her, in his usual pompous manner, but as gently as he could manage, "Why are you looking for your husband, madam?"

Sighing in relief, Zaya said calmly, "I have come from On, after I lost my means of livelihood there. I want him to know, sir, that I am now here."

The inspector gazed at the child that she held in her arms,

then asked her in the fashion of high-ranking persons, "Is that really why you came here—or was it to inform him of this child's birth?"

Zaya's cheeks flushed a deep red with shame. The man stared lustfully at her for an instant, before saying, "Fine . . . from what town is your husband?"

"From On, sir, but he was born in Thebes."

"And what is his name, madam?"

"Karda son of An, sir."

The inspector called for a scribe, dictating an order to him in the imperious style that he had earlier relinquished for the sake of Zaya's eyes.

"Karda son of An from On," he told him.

The scribe went to search in the record books, pulling out one and unrolling its pages, looking up the sign "k" and the name "Karda." He then returned to his chief, leaning into his ear and whispering in a low voice, before going back to his work.

The inspector regained his former demeanor and looked at the woman's face for some time, before saying quietly, "Madam, I am sorry that I must offer you my condolences for your husband. He died on the field of work and duty."

When the word "died" struck Zaya's ears, a scream of horror escaped her. Dazed, she paused for a moment, then asked the inspector in agonized entreaty, "Is my husband Karda really dead?"

"Yes, madam," he answered with concern. "In these situations, one can only try to endure it."

"But . . . how did you know it, sir?"

"This is what the scribe told me, after he searched through the names of the workers from On."

"Isn't it reasonable, sir, that his eyes could have deceived him?" she remonstrated. "Names can be similar."

The inspector asked for the scroll to be brought to his

desk. He looked through it himself, then shook his head regretfully. He glanced at the woman's face, which terror had tinged with the pallor of death. Noting a final glint of denial in the reluctant widow's eyes, he told her, "You must try to bear up, madam—and submit to the will of the gods."

The faint light of hope was extinguished. Zaya burst into tears, and the inspector demanded a chair for her. "Have courage, my good woman, have courage," he kept telling her. "This is what the gods have decreed."

Still, hope loomed before Zaya like a mirage to someone thirsting in the desert.

"Is it not possible, sir, that the deceased was a stranger who bore the same name as my husband?"

"Karda son of An was the only one to be martyred among the workmen from On," he said with certainty.

The woman moaned meekly and with pain.

"How awful my luck is, sir—can't the Fates find another target for their arrows other than my poor breast?" she said.

"Don't take it too hard," he urged.

"I have no other man but him, sir."

The good-hearted inspector wanted to reassure her when he said, "Pharaoh does not forget his faithful servants. His mercy covers the victims and the martyrs alike. Listen to me: our lord the king has ordered that houses be built for the families of laborers who meet their fate in the course of their work. They were built on the slope of the plateau, and many women and children dwell within them, whom the monarch provides with a monthly stipend. His will has decreed the selection of men from among their relatives to serve in the guards. Do you have a male relation that you would like to have appointed to watch over the workmen?"

"There is no one for me in the world but this child," replied Zaya, tearfully.

"You two will live in a clean room," he said, "and you will not know the humiliation of being questioned about it."

And so Zaya left the office of the pyramid's inspector a wretched widow, weeping for her husband's misfortune—and her own.

8

The houses that Pharaoh ordered built for the families of the martyred workmen were located outside the White Walls of Memphis, east of the Sacred Plateau. They were of modest size, with two stories, four spacious rooms on each level. Zaya and her child dwelt in one of these chambers. She grew accustomed to living among these widows and bereaved mothers and children, some of whom went on mourning their dead without ceasing. Others' wounds had healed, time having treated their sorrows. As a group, they were busy. Everyone had something to do: the young boys fetched water for the workmen, while the women sold them cooked food and beer. The wretched quarter was transformed into a burgeoning, low-priced bazaar filled with the bustle of ceaseless construction that announced its future as a prosperous town.

Zaya had spent her first days in her new home in constant sorrow, weeping for her lost husband. Her grief did not lessen, no matter what material blessings or sympathy she received that Bisharu, inspector of the pyramid, gave her. What a pity! For if only those suffering from loss would remember that Death is a void that effaces memory, and that the sorrows of the living vanish at the same speed with which the dead themselves disappear, how much toil and torment they could avoid for themselves! Yet, she grew stronger as the hardships of life made her forget the bitterness of death. But because of all the grumbling in her new home, after a few months she became convinced that it was not the right place for her or her son. Seeing no way out, however, she endured it in silence.

During these months, Inspector Bisharu visited her a number of times, whenever he went to these residences to check on their conditions. In fact, he visited many widows, but showed Zaya a distinctive degree of warmth and compassion. Though it is doubtful that others were less unfortunate than Zaya, none had hot, honey-colored eyes like Zaya's, nor a lithe, slender form like hers. Reflecting on his interest, Zaya said to herself, "What a fine man! True, he's short and fat, with coarse features, and at least forty years old or more—but he's so good-hearted, and so deeply loving as well!" With her secret eye she saw that when he looked at her supple figure his heavy eyelids fluttered and his thick lips shook. He became humble in place of his old arrogance, and when she traded pleasantries with him, he would be nailed where he stood like a boar impaled on a pike.

Her ambitions awakened, she unsheathed her secret weapon to conquer the great inspector. This happened when she took the opportunity of his presence to bewail her loneliness and gloom in her unhappy home.

"Perhaps I would be more useful, sir, in some other place, for I served a long time in the mansion of one of the good families of On," she told him. "I have great experience in the work of female servants."

The inspector's eyelids ceased trembling. "I understand, Zaya," he said, looking greedily at the gorgeous widow. "You don't complain out of indolence, yet—since you're used to the luxury of grander houses—your existence here must be dreadful."

The sly one essayed a coquettish smile, as she exposed the beautiful face of Djedef. "Will this place do for so lovely a child?"

"No," said the inspector. "Nor for you, Zaya."

Blushing, she let her eyelids drop until their lashes touched the hollows of her cheeks.

"I have the palace that you desire," the man said, "and— just perhaps—the palace desires you, too."

"I await but a sign, sire."

"My wife has died, leaving me two sons. I have four slave girls—would you, Zaya, be the fifth?"

On that very day, Zaya and Djedef moved from their squalid room to the women's quarters of the dazzling palace of Bisharu, inspector of the pyramid, whose garden went all the way out to the channel connecting to the Nile. She moved to his palace like a true slave girl—but with a status like no other. The atmosphere there was susceptible to her tricks and magical spells, for the house was without an effective mistress. Because the inspector's two sons were such little darlings, she used them to work on the sweet side of her master's character. Her campaign succeeded so well that she seduced him into marrying her. Soon the inspector's new wife took charge of the palace, and of raising his two boys, Nafa and Kheny. With no further need of deceit, once she rose to her high position, she swore to herself that she would give his two youngsters a proper upbringing, and to be for them a truly upstanding mother.

This is how Destiny smiled upon Zaya after a great reversal of fortune, and the world offered her a new life entirely, after her disaster.

9

Here was the palace that the Fates had determined would be the childhood home of Djedefra. For the first three years—as was the custom in Egypt in those days—he did not leave his mother's embrace unless it was time to sleep. During those three years, he touched Zaya's heart in a way that would not be erased for the rest of her life. Mothering and nurturing him filled her with fondness and compassion, yet we can do no more than scratch the surface when we discuss Djedef's early upbringing. After all, it was—like all childhoods—a locked-away secret, a kind of ecstasy in a bottle—whose essence is known only to the gods, and which they guard. The most that one could say is that he shot up quickly, like the trees of Egypt under the rays of her resplendent sun. His personality blossomed to reveal its goodness, like the rose when the warmth of life pierces its stalk, breathing into it the soul of beauty. He was Zaya's happiness, the light of her eyes, and it was the favorite game for Nafa and Kheny to snatch him away from one another and kiss him, and to teach him names, how to speak, and how to walk. But he finished his early childhood with knowledge that should not be dismissed lightly, for he knew how to call to Zaya, "Mama!" and she taught him to call Bisharu "Papa!" The man heard him say this with joy. He took as a good omen the boy-child's beauty, blessed with the splendor of the lotus. His mother also incessantly taught him to love the name of Ra. She demanded that he say it before going to bed, and when he awoke, in order to make the Lord's feelings flow for His dear son.

At three years of age, Djedef abandoned Zaya's embrace and began to crawl around his mother's room, and to walk, leaning on the chairs and couches, between the reception hall and the private chambers. An impulse to examine the pictures on the cushions, the decorations on the furniture legs, the paintings on the walls, the exquisite works of art strewn about, as well as the hanging lamps, guided him. His hand reached out for whatever it could grab, as he kept extending his grasp for the precious pleasure of it until, tiring of the effort, he would cry out, "Ra!" Or he would exhale a deep "Ah!" from his tiny chest, before resuming his mission of search and discovery. The inspector gave him a great wealth of toys: a wooden horse, a little war chariot, a crocodile with a gaping mouth. He lived with them in a little world of his own, where he made life as he wished it, where he would say that something would be—and it would be. The wooden horse, the war chariot, the gaping-mouthed crocodile each had its own life and ambitions. He spoke to them—and *they* spoke to *him*. He gave them orders—and they would obey, all the while sharing with him the secrets of inanimate things normally hidden from grown-ups.

At that time, a puppy named Gamurka was born in the palace to pedigreed parents of the old, venerable breed from Armant. Djedefra loved him at first sight, and brought him into his own room to live. The bond between them became indissoluble in that early age. Indeed, it was fated that Djedef would love Gamurka so much that he would actually grow up in his embrace, and that Djedef would watch over him in his sleep like his shadow. And that he would say his name, "Gamurka," sweetly on his tongue, and that the puppy's first bark was in calling out to him, and the first time that he wagged his tail was in greeting him. But sadly, Gamurka's

own infancy was not quite free of troubles—for the crocodile with the gaping mouth was lying in ambush for him.
When Gamurka saw this monster, he would begin to bark,
his eyes flashing, his body stiff with fright as he ran back
and forth, not calming down until Djedef put his fearsome
toy away.

The two hardly separated, for when Djedef went to bed,
Gamurka would lay by his side. If Djedef sat quietly—which
happened rarely—the puppy, legs akimbo, stretched out
across from him. Or he would keep licking his companion's
cheeks and hands, as his love required. He followed the boy
about in his walks in the garden, or rode with him in the
boat if Zaya carried him to it to tour about the palace pond.
They would raise their heads over the boat's rim to gaze at
their reflections in the water. As they stared, Gamurka
would not stop yapping, while Djedef delighted at the beautiful little creature that looked so much like him, who dwelt
in the pond's depths.

When spring came, the heavens were filled with the
hymns of the birds, cleaving the heavy mantle of winter that
had cloaked the joyous sun. The universe donned the festive
garb of youth—the trees in brocades of silk, the shrubs with
colorful flowers and their fragrances. Love was in the air,
and many couples amused themselves by boating, while
children were left to run about all but naked. Kheny and
Nafa leapt about in the water, swimming and throwing a
ball back and forth to each other. Djedef would stand with
Gamurka, watching them enviously—and would ask his
mother if he could do what they were doing. Then she
would lift him up from under his arms, setting him in the
water up to his waist, and he would kick with his feet,
shouting with glee and happiness.

When they had sated themselves with frolic and games,
they would return all together to the summer garden. Zaya
would sit on the couch and in front of her would be Djedef,

Kheny, and Nafa, and before them would lie Gamurka, again with his legs akimbo.

She would tell them the story of the shipwrecked sailor who floated over the crashing waves on a plank of wood to a lost island. She told them how the giant serpent who ruled the island had appeared to him, and how it would have killed him—if it hadn't realized that he was a faithful believer of praiseworthy conduct, as well as one of Pharaoh's subjects. The serpent looked after him, giving him a ship filled with precious treasures, with which the sailor returned to his homeland safe and sound.

Djedef didn't really understand these tales, but he eagerly followed their telling with his two beautiful dark eyes. He was happy and well loved, for who could not adore Djedef for those two deep black orbs, his long, straight nose, and his light, laughing spirit? He was loved when he spoke and when he did not, when he played and when he sat still, when he was content and when he was restless. He lived like the immortals, never worried about tomorrow.

But when he reached his fifth birthday, life began to reveal to him some of its secrets. At that time Kheny turned eleven years old, and Nafa, twelve. They finished their first level of schooling. Kheny chose to enter the School of Ptah to progress through its various levels, studying religion and morals, science and politics, because the youth—who had a natural leaning toward these subjects—aimed someday for a religious post, or perhaps a judgeship. Nafa, however, did not hesitate before enrolling in Khufu's school of fine arts, for he loved to fill his time with painting and engraving.

There came the time for Djedef to enter elementary school, and for four hours each day, the world of dreams in Zaya's room with Gamurka would be banished. He spent these hours with children and strangers, learning how to read and write, how to do sums, how to behave, and to love his homeland.

The first thing that they all heard on the first day was, "You must pay attention completely. Whoever doesn't should know that a boy's ears are above his cheeks—and he listens very closely once they've been smacked."

And for the first time in Djedef's life the stick played a part in his instruction, even though he got off to a good start by appearing well prepared to learn. He avidly applied himself to the beautiful language of the hieroglyphs, and quickly excelled in addition and subtraction.

Thanks to his strong and loveable personality, the teacher of morality and ethics had a profound influence upon him. He had a beguiling smile that fanned infatuation and confidence within the students' souls. What made Djedef love him even more was that he resembled his father Bisharu in his huge girth, his great jolly jowls, and his gruff, resounding voice. Djedef would lean toward him, utterly captivated, as the teacher said, "Look at what our sage Kagemni says—may his spirit in the heavens be blessed—when he tells us: 'Do not be stubborn in disputes, or you will earn the punishment of the Lord.' Also, 'That lack of courtesy is stupidity and a reproach.' Or, 'If you are invited to a banquet, when the best food is offered to you, do not covet it nor undertake to eat it, for people will think ill of you. Let a swallow of water suffice for your thirst, and a bite of bread be enough for your hunger.'" Afterward, he would interpret these sayings for the children, then recite proverbs as well as stories to them. Often he would admonish, "Don't let the infant within you forget what strenuous chores your mother endures for the sake of your fun. She bears you in her womb for nine months, then she holds you close to her for three years, feeding you with her milk. Do not annoy her, for the Lord hears her complaints, and answers her pleas."

Djedef would lean toward him, utterly rapt, savoring his sayings and his tales, totally under his sway. His primary education lasted seven years, in which he learned the basics of science, and became adept at reading and writing.

During this period, the fondness between him and his brother Nafa took strong root. He would sit with him while he painted and made drawings, following with his bewitching eyes the meandering lines that he traced, which together made the most beautiful shapes and the most creative works of art. All the while, Nafa possessed his heart with his never-ending laughter, his playful air, and his disarming pranks.

Kheny, though, had a clear influence over his mind. His budding knowledge continued to transcend basic principles, plumbing theology and the higher sciences at this precocious age. Because he found Djedef's handwriting pleasing, Kheny would dictate to him the notes from his lectures, enlightening his young mind with quotations from the wisdom of Kagemni, insights from the Book of the Dead, and spells from the poetry of Taya. All of this gently penetrated Djedef's immature mind, but with an aura of vague obscurity that awoke him from his innocence into a state of confused and uneasy wonder about life.

He loved Kheny, despite his gloomy gravitas, and whenever he allowed himself time to play, Djedef and Gamurka would race to his room. Djedef would also write down his lectures for him, or leaf through books adorned with pictures. In his childish way, he contemplated Ptah, Lord of Memphis, and his long staff with a curved end, bearing three signs—for strength, life, and immortality—and the image of Apis, the sacred bull, in which the spirit of Divine Ptah resides. Meanwhile, he would pelt Kheny with questions, which the older boy would answer patiently. Kheny also told to him the great Egyptian myths—it was extraordinary how they held him in thrall! In rapt attention, Djedef would sit squatting on his heels on the ground, leaning toward his brother, with Gamurka in front of him. His canine friend's face was turned toward him, giving his back to the teacher and his holy fables.

The carefree stage of childhood came to an end. Djedef lived it to the full, and more, yet his mind had grown beyond his age. He was like a young flowering tree, its branches covered in bloom—yet still no taller than the span of a few hands!

1 0

Time, sadly, moves always onward—never turning back! And as it moves, it delivers the destiny decreed for each person, executing its will—whose alteration and exchange are the sole comic diversion easing the boredom of eternity. From it comes all that time decays, and all that is renewed; all that revels in youth, and all that moans with age unto its final demise.

Time had done what it does to the family of Bisharu.

The man himself was now fifty. His corpulent body had started to sag, white hair covering his head, as bit by bit, he began to lose his strength, his youth, and his energy. His nerves were on edge as he shouted and yelled, scolding the guards and rebuking the scribes more and more often. Yet he was like the Egyptian bull, which bellows loudly even when not in pain, for his nature had two qualities that it never relinquished, that would not submit to the rule of time. These were his sense of honor and the goodness of his heart. After all, he was the inspector for the construction of Khufu's pyramid: woe be to whoever dared talk to him directly, if he were not of similar title or rank. He talked about himself tirelessly, as much as he could—and nothing so pleased him as the chatter of sycophants and flatterers.

And if he were summoned to appear before Pharaoh because of his position, his criers spread the news everywhere that his influence reached, so the people of his house, big and small, as well as his friends and subordinates would hear of it. Nor was that enough, for he would tell Nafa, Kheny, and Djedef, "Go broadcast the glorious news among your brothers, and let you little ones compete in telling of the honor that your father has attained by his loyal work and high talent." Yet he remained the good-hearted man he had always been—loathe to cause anyone harm, and whose anger never went beyond the tip of his tongue.

Zaya had now turned forty, yet the years showed little upon her. She kept her beauty and her freshness, while becoming a highly respected lady, thanks to her deep-rooted virtues. Indeed, whoever saw her living in Bisharu's palace would not imagine that she could ever have been the wife of Karda the laborer, and servant of the Lady Ruddjedet. She not only wrapped the memories of the past in the shrouds of forgetfulness, she forbade her memory from ever approaching that history enfolded in time. She wanted only to savor the main reason for her happiness—her motherhood of Djedef. In truth, she loved him as though she had actually borne him for nine months within her, and it was her dearest hope to see him grow to be a noble, contented man.

At that time, Kheny had passed through the longest phase of his advanced training; only three years remained for him to master his specialty. Since by nature he tended toward study and deep immersion in the secrets of the universe, he chose theology and the path that led to the priesthood. The matter was not entirely of his own choice—for the priesthood was a forbidding discipline whose doors are barred to all but those who merit it. He would first have to complete his final studies, then endure tests and trying duties for several years in one of the temples. But Kheny the student was received sympathetically when he showed both acute intelligence and noble ethics in his scholarly life, as though he inherited from his father only his gruff, raucous voice. Slender and sharp featured, of a calm demeanor, his traits called more to mind his mother, who was marked with godliness and piety.

In that, he was the exact opposite of his brother Nafa, who had his father's heavyset figure, full face, and his many-layered character. Gentle and easygoing, to his good fortune his features had emerged finer than Bisharu's thick and coarse ones. Finishing his studies, he was a certified master of painting and drawing, and—with his father's assistance—he rented a small house on the street named after King Sneferu, the most important commercial road in Memphis. This became his studio, where he made and displayed his artistic creations, and composed a sign in immaculate hieroglyphs that he hung outside, which read: "Nafa, son of Bisharu, Graduate of the Khufu School of Fine Arts." He continued to work and dream, patiently awaiting the crowds of buyers and admirers.

Nor was Gamurka spared the effects of time, for as he grew large, his long black coat became short. His face looked tough and strong, and his fangs warned of cruelty and the infliction of pain. His voice turned rough and gravelly; when he barked it echoed so fiercely that it spread terror in the hearts of cats, foxes, and jackals alike, announcing to all that the protector of the inspector's house was on guard. But for all his size and raw vitality, he was gentler than the breeze with his dear companion Djedef, with whom the ties of affection grew closer and closer with each passing day. When the boy called him, he came; when he gave him a command, he obeyed; and if he scolded him, he cowered and quieted down. He and Djedef also exchanged confidential messages by means other than language—for Gamurka would know when Djedef was approaching the house through a hidden sense, and would rush up to meet him when he saw him. The dog grasped what was inside the boy with a rare, amazing power that sometimes even the people closest to him lacked. He knew when he was ready for fun:

he would kiss him playfully, jumping up to lay both his forepaws on the youth's loincloth. He also knew his master's moments of fatigue or annoyance: then he would lie silently between Djedef's feet, and content himself with wagging his tail.

Now the boy had attained the age of twelve. The time had come for him to choose that to which he would devote his life. In truth, just a little while before, he had not thought at all about this dangerous question. Until now, the young man had shown a praiseworthy interest in everything, even deceiving Kheny with his passion for philosophy until the older boy was sure the priesthood was his only possible future. But Nafa—whose love of art ruled his sight—would watch him as he swam, as he ran, and as he danced. He saw his burgeoning body and his trim form, saying to himself when he imagined him dressed in military clothes, "What a soldier he'd make!" Thanks to their mutual affection, Nafa had a great influence on Djedef. As a result, he pointed him in the direction that Zaya most wanted for him. From that day onward, nothing so attracted Zaya during the popular festivals as the sight of soldiers, horsemen, and detachments of the army.

Bisharu did not concern himself with which art or science Djedef would choose to practice in life, for he had not meddled at all in Kheny or Nafa's choices for their own careers. But he was inclined to speculate, so he said, while all of them were sitting in the summer salon, and as he softly rubbed his massive belly, "Djedef—Djedef who only yesterday was still crawling instead of walking. Djedef has worked his little head very hard thinking about an appropriate choice for his career to pursue as a responsible adult. Time has come and gone, so please be compassionate, O Time, with Bisharu, and bear with him until the building of the pyramid is complete, for you will not find an effective replacement for him."

Declaring her own wish, Zaya said, "There is no need for a lot of questions. For whoever gazes upon Djedef's handsome face, his towering stature, and his upright bearing would have no doubt that he is looking at an officer of Pharaoh's charioteers."

Djedef smiled at his mother, whose speech had affirmed his own passion—recalling the squadron of chariots that he saw cutting through the streets of Memphis one day during the Feast of Ptah. They rode in tightly ordered parallel ranks, the charioteers in the vehicles standing erect, neither leaning to the side nor bobbing up and down, like imposing, immovable obelisks—drawing all eyes ineluctably toward them.

But Kheny was not satisfied with Zaya's choice, saying in his viscous voice, which resembled that of his father, "No, Mother, Djedef is a priest by temperament."

"I regret thwarting your desire this time, my brother," he continued. "How often has he made clear to me his readiness to learn and his inclination toward science and knowledge? How often have I been pressed to answer his many clever and intelligent questions? His preferred place is Ptah's academy, not the college of war. What do you think, Djedef?"

Djedef was brave and forthright on this occasion, not hesitating to express his opinion. "It upsets me that I must disappoint your hope this time, my brother," he said, "but the truth is that I wish to be a soldier."

Kheny was dumbfounded, but Nafa, laughing aloud, told Djedef, "You chose well—you look like nothing if not a soldier. This satisfies my own imagination. If you had chosen another discipline in life, you would have been so bitterly disappointed that it would have shaken your trust in yourself."

Bisharu shrugged his shoulders disdainfully. "It's all the same to me if you choose the army or the priesthood," he averred. "In any case, you have several months ahead of you to reflect on the subject. Oh, come on then, my sons! I imag-

ine that none of you will follow in your father's footsteps—
that not one of you will take on such a momentous role as I
have fulfilled in life."

The months went by without any change in Djedef's decision. But during this time, Bisharu faced a severe mental crisis, which his alleged fatherhood of Djedef had set in train.
In confusion he asked himself, "Should I continue to claim
this fatherhood, or has the time come to proclaim the truth
and to sever its bonds? Kheny and Nafa know the facts of
the matter, though they absolutely never refer to it, either in
private or in public, out of love for the boy, and in order to
spare him distress."

As Bisharu calculated the impact of this shock on the
blameless spirit of the happy youth, his ample torso shuddered. When he recalled Zaya, and what he would endure of
her anger and resentment, he flinched in apprehension. Yet
he did not think of this out of ill will or indifference to
Djedef, but because he believed that the reality would some-
how announce itself, if he did not do so first himself. Indeed,
the very best thing would be to reveal it now and be done
with it, rather than to hold it back until Djedef grew up,
thus doubling the torment it would cause him. The good
man hesitated, leaving the matter unresolved—and when it
was time to reach a decision before enrolling Djedef in the
military academy, he confided his secret thoughts to his son
Kheny.

But the matter horrified the young man, who told his
father in deep pain and sadness, "Djedef is our brother, and
the affection that binds us is stronger even than that
between brothers by blood. What harm would it do you,
father, if you let things be as they will be, rather than take
the dear boy by surprise with this unexpected blow of disgrace and humiliation?"

The one thing that could cost Bisharu due to his adoptive
fatherhood of Djedef was his inheritance. But of the vanities

of this world, Bisharu possessed no more than a substantial salary and a grand palace, and his paternity—or lack thereof—of Djedef threatened neither of these. For this reason, he sympathized with Kheny's anger, saying in self-defense, "No, my son, I would never humiliate him; I have called him my son, and I will continue to do so. His name will be inscribed among the students of the military college, 'Djedef son of Bisharu.'"

Then he laughed in his usual way, rubbing his hands as he said, "I've gained a son in the army."

Wiping away a tear that ran down his cheek, Kheny rejoined, "No—you've earned the Lord's pleasure, and His pardon."

11

The month of Tut was nearly done, and with it, only a few days remained for Djedef to stay in Bisharu's house before his departure to study the ways of war. These days were also the most nervous ones for Zaya. As she considered the two long months that he would be secluded within the academy—and then the long years that she would only be able to rest her eyes on him for a single day per month—fits of absentminded confusion overwhelmed her. The sight of his beautiful face and the sound of his beloved voice would be denied her, and with them the confidence and well-being that his nearness instilled in her. How brutal life can be! Sorrow enshrouded her long before the reasons for it would come to pass. Enfolding layers of pain oppressed her, like the waves of clouds driven by the winds amidst the fog of the dark and gloomy months of Hatur and Kiyahk.

When the cock crowed at dawn on the first day of the month of Baba, Zaya awoke and sat on her bed, muddled with sadness. An impassioned sigh was her first greeting to this day from the world of sorrows. Then she abandoned her bed and walked lightly to Djedef's little room to wake him and to dote over him. She entered the chamber on the tips of her toes in order not to disturb him, and Gamurka greeted her while stretching. But her plan was dashed when she found the youth had already awoken without her assistance. Softly he was singing a hymn, "We are the children of Egypt; we are descended from the race of the gods." The boy had risen by himself, obeying the first call of soldiery. From her heart, she cried out to him, "Djedef!" Slowly becoming aware of her, he then ran toward her like a bird greeting the morning's light, hanging from her neck and lifting his mouth toward her. She kissed him while he kissed her cheeks, and picked him up in her arms and kissed his legs, before carrying him outside saying, "Come and say goodbye to your father."

They found Bisharu still deeply asleep, sending up jarring snorts and grunts as he slumbered. She shook him with her hand until he sat upright, moaning, "Who's there? Who's there? Zaya?"

"Don't you want to say goodbye to Djedef?" she laughed as she shouted at him.

He sat in his bed, rubbing his eyes, then peered at the youth in the weak light of the lamp. "Djedef, are you going?" he said. "Come here and let me kiss you. Go now, in the protection of Ptah!"

He kissed him with his great, coarse lips once more, then added, "You are a child now, Djedef, but you're going to grow into a skillful soldier. I predict this for you, and the predictions of Bisharu, servant of Pharaoh, are never wrong. Go then safely, and I'll pray for your sake in the Holy of Holies."

Djedef kissed his father's hands, then went out with his mother. In the outer parlor, he met Kheny and Nafa standing there ready. Nafa cackled as he scolded him, "Hey, fearless warrior, the wagon is waiting!"

Zaya's face was transformed by yearning. Djedef lifted his face toward hers, filled with happiness and love. But alas, the months had passed fleetingly, and the time had come to say goodbye. Not embracing, nor kissing, nor weeping could lessen the tribulation. He descended the staircase between his two brothers and secured his place in the vehicle beside them. Then the wagon set off, carrying the dear one away as she gazed long after it through the mist of her tears—until it was swallowed by the blue light of dawn.

The wagon arrived at the military academy in Mereapis, the most beautiful suburb of mighty Memphis, with the rising of the sun. Yet they found the square in front of the school already crammed with boys hoping to enroll, all accompanied by one or more relatives. Each of them waited his turn to be called for scrutiny, after which he remained inside the academy—or was sent back whence he came.

That morning, the square was like a fairground, filled with festively decorated horses and sumptuous vehicles— for only the sons of the officer caste, or of the wealthy, were admitted to the college of war. Djedef turned anxiously right and left as he looked around, yet the faces he saw weren't strange to him, for many of those present were his classmates from primary school. So, pleased and charged with courage, his sagging spirits revived.

The voice of the school's crier called out continuously, while the torrent of students kept pouring into the building's monumental entrance. Some of them stayed within, while others emerged, their faces dejected, in obvious distress.

Kheny was staring sternly into the crowd. "Are you mad at me?" Djedef asked, disturbed by his look.

Kheny put his hands on the boy's shoulders. "May the Lord protect us, dear Djedef," he said. "The military is a sacred profession so long as it is just a public duty to which one devotes its full due for a time, and then returns to normal life. The soldier would not neglect any god-given talent, and would guard his spirit against useless distraction. I am confident, Djedef, that you will not disappoint any of the hopes that inflamed your soul in my room. As for your military escapade, and your commitment to carry it out—this entails the renunciation of your human feelings, the destruction of your intellectual life, and a regression back to the ranks of the animals."

Nafa laughed, as usual. "The truth is, my brother, you are rhapsodizing the pure life of wisdom, that of the priests," he said. "As for my own models, I sing the praises of beauty and pleasure. There are others—and these are the soldiers—who resent contemplation and worship sheer force. Mother Isis be praised that she endowed me with a mind that can perceive beauty in each of the colors that cover all things. Yet, in the end, I am not able to look after anyone's life but my own. In truth, the capacity to choose between these lives comes only to those who know them both, who are not biased against either one of them. But it's impossible to find such an arbiter."

Djedef's wait was not long, for soon the school crier called out, "Djedef son of Bisharu," and his heart pounded. Then he heard Nafa say to him, "Farewell, Djedef, for I don't think you'll be returning with us today."

The youth embraced his brothers and strode through the forbidding door. He went into a room to the right of the entrance, and was met by a soldier who ordered him to remove his clothes. The boy took off his robe and walked up to an elderly, white-bearded physician, who examined each limb and member, glancing appraisingly at his form. Then the doctor turned to the soldier and said, "Accepted." Overcome with joy, the boy put his robe back on, as the soldier led him out into the academy's courtyard, leaving him to join those who had been accepted before him.

The school's grounds were as vast as a large village, surrounded on three sides by a huge wall, adorned with warlike scenes of battlefields, soldiers, and captives. On the fourth side were barracks, storehouses for weapons and provisions, plus the headquarters for the officers and commanders, grain sheds, and sheds that housed the chariots and wagons, altogether resembling a formidable fortification.

The youth looked over the place in astonishment, his eyes eventually fixing on the assembled throng of his fellows. He found them puffing themselves up with tales of their family lineages, boasting of the exploits of their fathers and grand-fathers.

"Is your father a military man?" one boy asked him.

Irked at the question, Djedef shook his head. "My father is Bisharu, Inspector of the King's Pyramid," he said.

Yet the boy's face showed that he wasn't impressed by the title of inspector. "My father is Saka, Commander of the Falcon Division of spearmen," he bragged.

Annoyed, Djedef withdrew from their conversation, pledging to his young self that he would triumph over them, and surpass them one day. Meanwhile, the process of exam-ining and selecting the students dragged on for three hours. Those who were accepted were kept waiting until finally an officer approached them from the direction of the barracks. He glanced at them sternly, then called out to them. "From this moment forward, you must put all anarchy behind you forever," he warned. "You will regulate yourselves with order and obedience. From now on, everything—including food, drink, and sleep—is subject to strict discipline."

The officer lined them up in single file, and marched them toward the barracks. He ordered them to enter one by one, and as they did, they passed by a small window in the great warehouse, where each one was handed a pair of sandals, a white loincloth, and a tunic. Then they were split up among different dormitories, each one holding twenty beds in two opposing rows. Behind each bed was a medium-sized wardrobe, on top of which was a sheet of papyrus stretched in a wooden frame, upon which it was demanded that each individual write his name in the sacred script.

They all felt they were in peculiar surroundings, a place run with rigid organization, that produced a spirit of rigor and toughness. The officer loudly ordered them to take off their familiar clothes and to don their military uniforms. Then he warned them not to venture out into the courtyard unless they heard the sound of the horn—and they all complied with this command. A rapid movement spread throughout the dormitories, the first military action that these young boys would carry out. They rejoiced in their white warriors' regalia, exulting as they put it on. And when the horn was sounded, they scurried nimbly to the courtyard, where the officers lined them up into two straight lines.

Thereupon appeared the academy's director, a senior officer with the rank of commandant. His uniform was hung with insignia and medals. He reviewed them with care, then stood before them as he declaimed: "Yesterday you were carefree children, but today you are beginning a life of dutiful manhood acted out through military struggle. Yesterday you belonged to your fathers and mothers, but today you are the property of your nation and your sovereign. Know that the life of a soldier is strength and sacrifice. Order and obedience are incumbent upon you, in order to fulfill your sacred obligation to Egypt and Pharaoh."

Then the director cheered in the name of Khufu, King of Egypt, and the little soldiers cheered as well. The man commanded them to sing the anthem, "O Gods, preserve Your son whom we worship, and his fortunate kingdom, from the source-spring of the Nile, unto its estuary." The great courtyard was filled with their birdlike voices, singing with a bursting enthusiasm and a magnificent beauty, invoking the gods, Pharaoh, and Egypt in a single melody.

That evening, when Djedef lay for the first time on this

strange bed in these alien surroundings, his loneliness would not let him sleep. He sighed from the depths of his being as his imagination wandered back and forth between the darkness of the dormitory and the happy vision of Bisharu's house. He felt as though he could see Zaya as she bent toward him, and Nafa laughing contentedly, and Kheny holding forth in his logical, but effusive fashion. His dearest thought was of Gamurka as the dog licked his cheek and greeted him with his wagging tail. And when he had lost himself in his dreams, his eyelids grew heavy as he fell into a deep slumber, from which he did not stir till the sound of the horn at dawn. He then sat up in his bed without any hesitation, staring around himself with surprise, watching his friends awake and overcome the power of sleep with difficulty. Their yawns and complaints filled the air, though they were also mixed with laughter.

There would be no play time after today, for the life of busyness—and battle—had begun.

1 3

During this time, the architect Mirabu asked for an audience with Pharaoh, and appeared before him in his official reception hall. His Majesty reposed on the throne of Egypt, which he had occupied for twenty-five years, performing the most glorious works for his country. He was frightful, resolute, and powerful, and a single glance did not suffice to take in all his grandeur, just as his fifty years of life had not been enough to weaken the solidity of his build or his exuberant vitality. And so he retained the sharpness of his vision, the blackness of his hair, and the acuity of his mind, as well.

Mirabu prostrated himself before him, kissing the hem of the royal robe. Pharaoh welcomed him with affection.

"Peace be upon you, Mirabu," he said. "Rise and tell me why you have come to see me."

The architect stood up before his master on the throne, his face beaming with joy, saying: "My lord, the granter of life and the source of light, my loyalty to your Sublime Self has permitted me to accomplish my majestic task, and to crown my service to you with this immortal monument. I now obtain in one happy hour what the man of faith wishes for with his belief, and what the artist wishes from his art. For the gods, upon whom each created being is dependent, have willed that I inform Your Adored Eminence of the good news that the mightiest construction ever undertaken in the land of the Nile since the age of creation, and the largest building on which the sun has risen in Egypt since the first time it rose over the valley, is now finished. I am certain, sire, that it will remain standing throughout the continuous generations to come, bearing your holy name, attesting to your magnificent epoch, preserving your divine spirit. It will proclaim the struggle of millions of Egyptian working hands, and scores of emminent minds. Today, for this work there is no peer, while tomorrow it will be the place of rest for the most glorious soul ever to rule over the land of Egypt. And after tomorrow—and for eternity—it will be the temple within whose expanse beat the hearts of millions of your worshippers, who will make their way to it both from North and South."

The timeless artist fell silent for a moment—then the king's smile encouraged him to continue.

"We celebrate today, my lord," he said, "Egypt's eternal emblem, and its truthful epithet, born of the strength that binds her North with her South. It is the offspring of the patience that overflows in all her children, from the tiller of the earth with his hoe, to the scribe with his sheet of papyrus. It is the inspiration for the faith that beats in the hearts of her people. It is the exemplar of the genius that has made our homeland sovereign over the earth, around which the sun floats in its sacred boat. And it shall remain forever the deathless revelation that settles in the hearts of the Egyptians—granting them strength, instilling them with patience, inspiring them with faith, and driving them to create."

The king listened to the architect with a smile of delight, his piercing eyes glistening, his face bursting with ecstatic enthusiasm. When Mirabu was finished, Pharaoh said, "I congratulate you, O Architect, on your unequaled brilliance. And I thank you for the magnificent work that speaks so highly of your king and country—for which we owe you appreciation and praise. We shall fete your mighty miracle with an awesome celebration—one fit for its immortal grandeur."

Mirabu bowed his head as he listened to Khufu's encomium, as he would to a divine hymn.

And hence, to inaugurate his awesome monument, Pharaoh held an official, popular ceremony, of stupendous proportions—during which the holy plateau beheld twice as many human beings as it had rugged laborers. Yet this time they did not bring with them hoes and other tools—rather, they carried banners, olive branches, palm fronds, and sprigs of sweet basil, as they sang the righteous sacred anthems. Among these throngs, the soldiers made a great thoroughfare that extended from the Valley of Eternity eastward, after which it circled around the pyramid—before ascending westward until it flowed once again into the valley. Along this road marched the bands of dignitaries as they circumambulated the gargantuan construction in procession. At their forefront were groups of priests from their various orders, followed by the nobles and the local chieftains. Then the troops of the army stationed in Memphis, both on horse and on foot, cut their way through the crowds. But after these, all eyes were drawn to Khufu and the princes: the worshipful masses swiveled their heads as the royal retinue passed, cheering their king from the depths of their hearts. As they did so, they seemed to lean forward as one, all in the same direction, as though assembled in prayer.

Pharaoh hailed the pyramid with a brief speech, then the vizier Hemiunu consecrated it with a blessing. This concluded, the king's cortege set off back to Memphis, and the high-level groups began to break up. As for the crowds of the common people, they kept circling the immense building in jubilation. Their ranks did not dissolve until the dawn poured down its splendor, its magical calm spreading over the green, gemlike surface of the valley.

That evening, Pharaoh invited the princes and his closest

companions to the private wing of his palace. As the weather was turning cool, he met them in his grand salon, where they reposed upon chairs made of pure gold.

Despite his brawn, the king's eyes showed the strain of the great responsibilities that weighed upon him. Though his outward aspect had not altered, it was obvious that the hardships of passing time had overpowered his inner being. This was not lost on his closest intimates, such as Khafra, Hemiunu, Mirabu, and Arbu. They noticed that Pharaoh was little by little becoming an ascetic, practicing nonphysical pursuits—no matter how much more manly activities, such as hunting and the chase, were dear to his heart. He now inclined toward gloomy contemplation and reading: sometimes the dawn would overtake him while he was sitting on his cushion, studying books of theology and the philosophy of Kagemni. His former sense of humor changed to sarcasm, replete with dark thoughts and misgivings.

The most amazing thing about that evening—and the least expected—was that the king should have displayed any sign of anxiety or distress whatsoever on this, of all nights, when he was marking the most monumental achievement in history. Of all the people with him, the one most aware of the king's unease was the architect Mirabu, who could not restrain the urge to ask him, "What so clearly preoccupies the mind of my lord?"

Pharaoh looked at him somewhat mockingly, and asked, as one wondering aloud, "Has history ever known a king whose mind was carefree?"

Thinking little of this answer, the artist went on, "But it is only right for my sire to rejoice this evening, without any reservation."

"And why is it right for your lord to rejoice?"

Mirabu was stunned into silence by the king's derisive reply, which almost made him forget the beauty of Pharaoh's praise and the grandeur of his celebration. But Prince

Khafra was not pleased with the psychological changes in the king.

"Because, my lord," he said, "we fete today the blessing of the greatest technical accomplishment in the long annals of Egypt."

Laughing, Khufu replied, "Do you mean my tomb, O Prince? Is it right for a person to exult over the construction of his grave?"

"Long may the God keep our lord among us," Khafra said, adding, "Glorious work merits rejoicing and recognition."

"Yes, yes—but if it reminds one of death, then there must also be a bit of sadness."

"It reminds us of immortality, my lord," said Mirabu, with passion.

"Do not forget, Mirabu," said Pharaoh, smiling, "that I am an admirer of your work. But the intimation of one's mortality fills the soul with grief. Yes, I do not dwell on what has inspired your magisterial monument with death-less profundity—rather, on the fact that immortality is itself a death for our dear, ephemeral lives."

Here Hemiunu interjected with staidness, reflection, and faith, "My lord, the tomb is the threshold to perpetual existence."

To this, the king replied, "I believe you, Hemiunu. Yet the coming journey requires considerable preparation—especially since it is eternal. But do not think that Pharaoh has any fear or regret—no, no, no—I am simply astonished by this mill-stone that keeps on turning and turning, grinding up kings and commoners alike each day."

Prince Khafra was growing annoyed with the king's philosophizing. "My lord spends too much time thinking," he said.

Knowing his son's nature, Pharaoh answered, "Perhaps, Prince, this doesn't please you."

"Forgive me, sire," said Khafra. "But the truth is that

contemplation is the task of the sages. As for those whom the gods submit to the tribulations of rule, it's no wonder that they seek to shun such difficult matters."

"Are you insinuating that I have toppled into the abyss of old age?" Khufu questioned him, jeeringly.

The companions grew alarmed. But the prince was the most alarmed of all. "The Lord forbid, my father!" he blurted.

Derisively, but with a strong voice, the king replied, "Calm yourself, O Khafra. Know that your father will retain his grip on authority with an iron hand."

"Then I am entitled, my lord," said Khafra, "to be gratified, though I have heard nothing new."

"Or do you think that the king is not a king unless he declares a war?" Khufu asked.

Prince Khafra was always pointing out to his father that he should send an army to chastise the tribes of Sinai. He grasped what Pharaoh was getting at, and was taken aback for a moment.

Hemiunu seized on this momentary silence. "Peace is more manly than war for the strong, upright king" he said.

The prince rejoined in a forceful tone that bespoke the hardness and cruelty traced upon his face, "But the king must not allow a policy of peace to prevent him from making war when the need to fight is serious!"

"I see that you're still dwelling on this ancient subject," Khufu remarked.

"Yes, sire," said Khafra, "nor will I desist till my view is accepted—for the tribes of Sinai are corrupting the land: they threaten the government's prestige."

"The tribes of Sinai! The tribes of Sinai!" Khufu bellowed. "The police are enough for now to take care of their little bands. As for dispatching the army to raid their strongholds, I feel that the conditions are not yet right for that. Note that the nation has just borne the immense effort that it undertook so benevolently in order to build Mirabu's pyramid. But there shall soon come a time when I will put an end to their evil, and I will protect the nation from their aggression."

A silence swept over them for a few moments, then the king ran his gaze back and forth among those present. "I have invited you this evening," he said, "to reveal to you the overwhelming desire that beats within my breast."

They all peered at him in fascination as he said, "This morning I asked myself, 'What have I done for the sake of Egypt, and what has Egypt done for my sake?' I will not conceal the truth from you, my friends—I found that what the people have done for me is double that which I have done for them. This to me was painful, and these days I have been very much in pain. I remembered the adored sovereign Mina, who endowed the nation with its sacred unity—yet the homeland gave him only a fraction of what it has granted me. So I humbled myself, and swore to repay the people for their goodness with goodness, and for their beauty with even more beauty."

Moved, Commander Arbu objected, "His Majesty the King has been harsh with himself in this accounting."

Ignoring Arbu's remark, Khufu resumed, "Though they aspire to be just and fair, monarchs are often oppressive. Though anxious to promote goodness and well being, they also do a great deal of harm. And with what deed, other than immortal good works, can they repent for their transgressions and expiate their sins? Thus, my pain has guided me to an immense and benevolent undertaking."

His companions gazed at him wonderingly, so he went on, "I am thinking, gentlemen, of composing a great book, in which I shall combine the proofs of wisdom and the secrets of medicine, with which I have been deeply enamored since childhood. In this way, I would leave behind me a lasting influence upon the people of Egypt, guiding their souls and protecting their bodies."

Mirabu shouted with boundless joy, "What a marvelous labor, my lord, by which you shall govern the people of Egypt forever!"

Pharaoh smiled at the architect, who reiterated, "One more will be added to our holy books."

Prince Khafra, weighing in his mind what the king wished to do, said, "But my lord, this is a project that will take many long years."

Arbu joined in his dissent, "It took Kagemni all of two decades to write his tome!"

But Pharaoh simply shrugged his broad shoulders. "I will devote to it what remains of my life," he said.

After a moment's silence, he asked, "Do you know, gentlemen, the place where I have chosen to compose my book, night after night?"

Khufu looked into their puzzled faces, then told them, "The burial chamber in the pyramid that we feted today."

Surprise and disbelief showing in their expressions, the king continued, "In worldly palaces the tumult of this fleeting life prevails. They are not suitable for creating a work destined for eternity!"

And with this, the audience ended—for Pharaoh did not like discussion when he had already fixed upon a final opinion. So his friends withdrew, during which time the heir apparent rode in his chariot along with his chief chamberlain, telling him with intense agitation, "The king prefers poetry to power!"

As for Khufu, he made his way to the palace of Queen Meritites, finding her in her chamber with the young Princess Meresankh, sister of Khafra, who was not yet more than ten years old. The princess flew toward him like a dove, happiness flashing in her lovely dark eyes. At the sight of Meresankh—she of the face like a full moon, with a golden brown complexion and eyes that could cure sickness with their cheer—Pharaoh could not help but smile lovingly. And so, his breast relieved of all sorrows and concerns, he greeted her with open arms.

1 4

An air of delight stirred within Bisharu's palace that night. Signs of it were plain in the laughing faces of both Zaya and Nafa—and that of the inspector himself. Even Gamurka seemed to sense that something good was coming, feeling deep inside that he should rejoice, for he raced around barking, rushing back and forth in the garden like a reckless arrow in flight.

They were all waiting expectantly, when suddenly they heard a clamor from without—as the loud voice of the servant cried out ecstatically, "My young lord!" At this, Zaya leaped to her feet and ran toward the staircase, flowing down the steps without looking left or right. And at the end of the entrance hall she saw Djedef in his white uniform and military headdress, shimmering like the rays of the sun. She threw wide her arms to embrace him—and found that Gamurka had beaten her to him. He assaulted his master excitedly, hugging him with his forepaws, yipping at him to complain of the agony of his yearning.

She pulled the dog aside and grasped her dear boy to her heart, smothering him with kisses. "The Spirit answered me, my son," she shouted. "Oh, how I have missed your eyes, and how upset I was with longing for the sight of your beautiful face. My darling, you've become so much thinner, and the sun has scorched your cheeks—you're worn out, dear Djedef!"

Drawn to the noise, Nafa came, laughing as he greeted his brother, "Welcome, Mighty Soldier!"

Djedef smiled, glancing between his mother and brother, while Gamurka danced enraptured in front of him, cutting ahead of his path on every side. Kissing his cheek, the inspector received him warmly. Bisharu looked at him for a long while with his bulging eyes that revealed his discernment.

"You have changed in these two months," he said. "You are now truly starting to show the marks of manhood. You missed the celebration for the great pyramid, but don't feel sorry for that, because I'll show it to you myself—for I am still, and will continue to be, the inspector for the area until I take my retirement. But why are you so tired, my child?"

Djedef laughed as he said, while playing about Gamurka's head, "Army life is cruel and harsh. During the whole day in the academy we are either running, swimming, or riding—now I'm an expert horseman!"

"May the gods preserve you, my son," said Zaya.

"Do you also throw spears or practice shooting arrows?" asked Nafa.

Djedef explained the school's regimen to his brother with the effusive prolixity of the fascinated pupil.

"No," he said, "in the first year, we train with games, and in horseback riding. In the second year, we learn fencing with swords, daggers, and javelins. In the third year, we drill with spears, and theoretical studies are thrust upon us. Then in the fourth year, we have archery, and history lessons as well. In the fifth year, we take up the war chariot, and finally, in the sixth year, we review the military sciences and visit fortresses and citadels."

"My heart tells me that I'll see you as a great officer, O Djedef. Your face inspires enthusiasm—and there's no harm in that, for in my calling, we predict people's futures from the nature of their features."

Then Djedef, as if suddenly remembering something very important, inquired with interest, "Where is Kheny?"

"Didn't you know that he has joined the ranks of the priests?" Bisharu answered for him. "They now keep him behind the walls of the Temple of Ptah. They are teaching him the religious sciences, along with ethics and philosophy, in total isolation—far from the din and distractions of the world. They are trained for a life that is the closest of all to that of the soldier—for they wash themselves twice by day, and twice by night. They also shave their heads and their bodies, wear garments of wool, and renounce the consumption of fish, pork, onion, and garlic. They must pass the toughest examinations, and instruct other people in the sacred secrets of knowledge. Let us all pray that the gods steady his steps, to make him a sincere servant for them, and for their faithful believers."

To this, all of them then said, as though with one breath, "Amen."

"So when shall I have the good fortune to see him?" asked Djedef.

"You won't see him for four years, the years of the greatest temptation," said Nafa, regretfully.

Djedef's face had darkened with sorrow and longing for his earliest mentor, when Zaya asked him, "How will we see you, from now on?"

"On the first of every month," the boy answered.

At this, her brow furrowed, but Nafa laughed, "Don't stir up sadness, Mother," he said. "Let's see how we can spend this day—what do you think of an outing on the Nile?"

Zaya shouted, "In Kiyahk?"

"Does our soldier dread the harshness of storms?" Nafa asked, sarcastically.

"But I can't do it in this month's weather," answered Zaya, instead. "Nor can I be separated from Djedef for even one minute of this day. So let's all stay in the house together. I have saved up a long talk with him that I cannot bear to keep to myself any longer."

Meanwhile, all of them had noticed that Djedef's formerly carefree spirit had disappeared, that he spoke but rarely, and that an unfamiliar stiffness and gravity now enfolded him. Nafa looked at him with surreptitious anxiety, and asked himself: "Will Djedef keep this new personality for very long? He's running away from seriousness and rigidity. Perhaps he didn't feel the loneliness in Kheny's absence when he was under the stress of his army discipline." But he denied his fears to himself, saying, "Djedef is still new to his military life. He's not able to digest all of it in just a short time. He'll feel some alienation and pain until he becomes accustomed to it completely. At that time he will put aside his unhappiness, and his normally jolly and pleasant nature will return." Then he thought that if Djedef accompanied him to look over his art, then perhaps his gaiety would revive. So he said to him, "Hey, Officer Big Shot, what do you think of going to see some of my pictures?"

But Zaya was furious. "Stop trying to steal him away from me!" she shouted. "On the contrary—for he's not leaving this house today!"

Nafa drew a deep breath and said nothing. Then a thought occurred to him. He produced a large sheet of papyrus and a reed pen, and said to his brother, "I will draw a portrait of you in this beautiful white outfit. This will help me keep the memory of this lovely occasion, so that I may look upon it fondly on the day your shoulders are adorned with a commander's insignia."

Thus the family spent a gorgeous day in entertaining chatter and other pleasures. Indeed, this visit became the model for each of Djedef's homecomings every month, that seemed to pass in the twinkle of an eye. Nafa's fears were dispelled, as the lad lost his stiffness, and his bold, playful self returned. His body reveled in its strength and manliness, as he progressed further and further on the road to developing his physical power and magnetism.

The summer—when the academy closed its doors—was the happiest time for Zaya and Gamurka. During these days, they became reaccustomed to the uproar of life and the activities that they all shared before the brothers split up into their different walks of life. The family often traveled to the countryside or to the northern Delta in order to go hunting, using a skiff to plow through the waves of lakes shaded by papyrus groves and lotus trees. Bisharu would stand between his boys Nafa and Djedef, each one holding his curved hunting stick, until a duck—not suspecting what Fate had in store for it—flew overhead, and each took aim at the target, throwing all his strength and skill into it.

An adroit hunter, Bisharu was twice as successful at it as his two sons combined. He would look sharply down at Djedef and say in his gruff voice, "Don't you see, soldier, how good your father is at hunting? Don't be so surprised—for your father was an officer in the army of King Sneferu, and was strong enough to capture a whole tribe of savages without fighting at all."

These sporting trips were a time of exercise and enjoyment unmatched on other occasions. Yet Bisharu's mind would not be at rest until he took Djedef on a visit to the pyramid. His goal from the beginning was to show off his influence and authority, and the kind of reception given him by the soldiers and employees there.

Meanwhile, Nafa invited Djedef to visit his gallery to show him his pictures. The youth was still working hard, with hardly any funds, hoping that he would one day be invited to take part in a worthy artistic project in one of the palaces of the wealthy or prominent. Or that one of his visitors should buy something. Djedef loved Nafa, and he loved his works of art—especially the picture that he drew of him in his white war uniform—which captured the essence of his features and the expression in his eyes.

At this time, Nafa was painting a portrait of the immortal architect Mirabu who had brought the greatest miracle of technical achievement into existence.

As he sketched the underlying drawing for the painting, he said to Djedef, "I have never put half as much into any painting as I have invested in this one. That's because, to me, the figure in this portrait has a divine character."

"Are you painting it from memory?" Djedef queried.

"Yes, Djedef," he replied, "for I never see the great artist except during feast days and official celebrations in which Pharaoh's courtiers appear. Yet that is enough to have engraved his image in my heart and mind!"

The year passed again, and Djedef went back to the academy once more. The wheel of time kept turning, as the life of Bisharu's family proceeded down its predestined path: the father into old age, the mother into maturity, Kheny into devotion to religion, Nafa into the perfection of his exquisite art. Meanwhile, Djedef made greater and greater strides toward an ingeniously superior mastery of the arts of war, gaining a reputation in the military academy never before attained by any pupil.

15

Djedef strolled down Sneferu Street as an unending stream of passersby stopped to gawk at his white military uniform, his tall, slender body, and his clean good looks. He kept walking until he came to the entrance of the house of "Nafa son of Bisharu," with its license from Khufu's school of drawing and painting. He read the name plaque with interest, as if he were seeing it for the first time, and on his delightful face there was a sweet, radiant smile. Then he passed through the doorway, and inside he saw his brother absorbed in his work, completely unaware of what was around him—so he called out to him laughingly, "Peace be upon you, O Great Maker of Images!"

Nafa swiveled toward him, a surprised look on his dreamy face. When he realized who had come, he rose to greet him, saying, "Djedef! What good fortune! How are you, man? Have you been to the house?" The two brothers embraced for a while, then Djedef said, as he sat on a chair that the artist had brought to him, "Yes, I was there, then I came to see you here—for you know that your house is my chosen paradise!"

Nafa laughed in his high-pitched way, his face overflowing with pleasure. "How happy I am with you, Djedef! I was amazed at how an officer such as you could be so drawn to this calm, idyllic place for painting! Where is Djedef of the battlefield, and of the forts of Per-Usir and Piramesse?"

"Don't be amazed, Nafa, for I truly am a soldier. But one who loves fine art, just as Kheny loves wisdom and knowledge."

Nafa's eyebrows shot upwards in shock, as he asked, "Imagine if you were heir apparent in the kingdom! Don't you see them grooming him for the throne, with education about wisdom, art, and war?" He continued, "A divine policy made Egypt's kings into gods—as it one day will make you a commander without peer."

The blood rose in Djedef's cheeks as he said, smiling, "You, Nafa, are like my mother—you don't see me even though you ascribe to me all of the best qualities combined!"

At this, Nafa let out his high, piercing laugh, seeming to drown in it for a long while, until he recovered his composure.

Astonished, Djedef asked him, "What's wrong with you? What's so funny about that?"

The young man, still giggling, replied, "I'm laughing, Djedef, because you compared me with your mother!"

"Well, what's funny about that? I just meant that . . ."

"Don't trouble to explain or excuse yourself, for I know what you meant by it," Nafa interrupted. "But that's the third time today that someone has likened me to a female. First, this morning, Father told me that I was 'as fickle as a girl.' Then, just an hour ago, the priest Shelba said to me, while he was talking to me about my doing a portrait of him, 'You, Nafa, are ruled by emotion, just as women are.' And now you come along, and say I'm like your mother! Well, do you see me as a man, or as a woman?"

Now it was Djedef's turn to laugh. "You are indeed a man, Nafa. But you are delicate of spirit, with a passionate sensitivity. Don't you remember Kheny once saying that 'artists are a sex between female and male?'"

"Kheny believed that art must borrow something from

femininity—yet I feel that the emotionality of a woman is in absolute contradiction to that of the artist. For by her nature, a woman is utterly efficient in reaching her biological objectives using every means at her disposal. Whereas the artist has no objective but to express the essence of things, and that is Beauty. For Beauty is the sublime essence of that which creates harmony among all things."

Again, Djedef laughed. "Do you think that by your philosophizing you can convince me that you're a man?"

Nafa fixed him with a sharp stare. "Do you still need proof?" he replied. "Well, then, you should know—I'm going to be married."

"Is what you say true?" Djedef asked, the incredulity plain on his face.

Nafa was practically drowning in laughter when he answered, "Has it reached the point where you would deny that I should get married?"

"Certainly not, Nafa," said Djedef, "but I remember how you made Father mad at you, by your abstention from marriage."

His face grown serious, Nafa placed his hand over his heart. "I fell in love, Djedef," he said. "I fell in love—very suddenly."

Djedef—his feelings now gathered in concentrated awareness—asked in concern, "Suddenly?"

"Yes, I was like the bird hovering safely in the sky until he feels an arrow dive into his heart—and he falls."

"When did this happen, and where?"

"Djedef, when one talks about love, you don't ask about the time and the place!"

"Who is she?"

He said with reverence, as though intoning the name of Isis, "Mana, daughter of Kamadi in the Office of the Treasury."

"And what will you do?"

"I will marry her."

Djedef wondered, in a dreamy voice, "Is this how things change?"

"And even faster than that," said Nafa. "An arrow and its victim—and what is the bird to do?"

Truly, love is an awesome thing. Djedef knew art, the teachings of the sages, and the sword. As for love, this was a new mystery indeed. And how could it not be a mystery, if it could do in one instant what Bisharu and he were unable to do in years! Meanwhile, he sensed his own passion flaring and his spirit wandering in far distant valleys.

"A happy Fate has willed that I be successful in my life as an artist, and Lord Fani invited me to decorate his reception hall. Some of my pictures were valued at ten pieces of gold—though I refuse to sell them. Look at this little one!"

Puzzled, Djedef turned toward where Nafa was pointing, and saw the miniature image of a peasant girl on the banks of the Nile, the horizons of evening tinged with the hues of sunset. As though awakened by the beauty of this picture that drew him from the valleys of his dreams, he approached it slowly, until he came to within an arm's length of it. Nafa saw his amazement and could not have been more pleased.

"Do you not see it as a picture rich in both color and shadow? Look at the Nile, and the horizons!" he exclaimed.

Djedef answered in an otherworldly voice, "Just ask me to look at the peasant girl!"

Contemplating her picture, Nafa said, "The brush has immortalized the flow of the Nile, which has such dignity."

But Djedef interjected, without paying any attention to what the artist was saying, "By the gods . . . such a soft, supple body, as slender and upright as a lance!"

"Look at the fields, and at the bent-over crops, whose direction shows . . ." said Nafa.

As though he didn't hear his brother at all, Djedef muttered: "How gorgeous this bronze face is, like the moon!"

". . . that the wind was blowing from the south!" continued Nafa.

"How beautiful these two dark eyes—they have such a divine expression!"

"Joy isn't all there is in this picture. Notice also the sunset—only the gods know how much effort I put into drawing and tinting it," said Nafa.

Djedef looked at him with a mad enthusiasm. "She's alive, O Nafa—I can almost hear her murmuring. How can you live with her under one roof?"

Nafa rubbed his hands happily. "For her sake, I turned down ten pieces of pure gold," he said.

"This painting will never be sold."

"And why is that?" asked Nafa.

"This picture is mine, even if I should pay for it with my life!"

Nafa said, laughing, "O age seventeen! You're like a blazing fire, a leaping flame. You give life and womanly qualities to stones, colors, and water. You passionately adore illusions and imaginings, and turn dreams into actualities . . . and you've brought us all the tortures of hell!"

The boy blushed, and fell silent. Nafa took pity on his exasperation, and said, "I am at your command, O Soldier."

"You must never part with this picture, O Nafa," said Djedef imploringly.

Nafa strode over to the picture, and lifting it from its place, presented it to his brother, saying, "Dear Djedef, she's yours."

Djedef held it gently with his hands, as though he were clasping his own heart, then said like one obliged to be grateful, "Thank you, Nafa!"

Nafa sat down contented. As for Djedef, he stuck to his place without budging, absorbed in the face of the divine peasant girl.

At length he said, "How does the creative imagination captivate one so?"

"She's not a creature of imagination," said Nafa, calmly.

The youth's heart quaked as he asked with desire, "Do you mean that the possessor of this form moves among the living?"

"Yes," Nafa answered.

"Is . . . is she like your image of her?"

"She is even more beautiful, perhaps."

"Nafa!" shouted Djedef.

The artist grinned, as the enraptured young man interrogated him, "Do you know her?"

"I have seen her at times on the banks of the Nile," he replied.

"Where?"

"North of Memphis," said Nafa.

"Does she always go there?"

"She used to go in the late afternoon with her sisters, and they would sit down and play and then disappear with the setting sun. I used to take my place hidden behind a sycamore fig tree—I could hardly wait for them to arrive!"

"Are they still going there?" asked Djedef.

"I don't know," replied Nafa. "I stopped following their movements when I had completed my picture."

Djedef looked at him doubtfully. "How could you?" he said.

"This is a beauty that I worship, but which I do not love."

Djedef, paying no attention to what Nafa was saying, asked him, "In what place did you see her?"

"North of the Temple of Apis."

"Do you think that she still goes there?" Djedef queried.

"And what, O Officer, prompts your question?"

A look of confusion flashed in Djedef's eyes, and Nafa asked him, "Could Fate have it that these two brothers are wounded by the arrow of love in the same week?"

Djedef frowned as he returned to regarding the picture thoughtfully.

"Don't forget that she's a peasant girl," said Nafa.

"Rather, she's a ravishing goddess," Djedef muttered back.

"Ah, Djedef, I was struck by the arrow and destroyed in the palace of Kamadi," said Nafa, laughing, "but I fear that you may be struck in a broken-down hut!"

16

The day bore the seal of dreams, as around midafternoon, Djedef—the enchanting portrait next to his breast—went to the bank of the Nile, rented a boat, and headed north. He was not truly aware of what he was doing, nor could he stop himself from doing it. Simply put, he had fallen under a spell and could submit only to its commands, and hear only its call. He set off in pursuit of his unknown objective driven by an all-conquering passion that he could not resist. This magic had seized a man for whom death held no terror, who had no regard for danger. Naturally, then, he struck out boldly for his goal, for it was not his custom to shrink back—and whatever would be, would be.

The boat made its way, cutting through the waters, propelled by the current and the youthful strength of his arms. All the while, Djedef kept his eyes fixed on the river's edge, searching for the object of his persistent quest. And what should he see first but the mansions of the wealthy people of Memphis, their marble staircases descending to the banks of the Nile. Beyond them, for many furlongs, he beheld the spreading fields until there appeared in the far distance Pharaoh's palace garden in the City of the White Walls. Djedef piloted his skiff in the midcourse of the river in order to avoid the Nilotic Guards, until—at the Temple of Apis—he turned back to shore once more. He then hastened northward opposite the spot, where people were not seen except during the great feasts and festivals. He would have given up in despair if he had not then noticed a group of peasant girls sitting on the riverbank nearby, dipping their legs into the flowing waters. His heart pounded intensely as his sense of bleakness fled, his eyes gleaming with ecstatic hope. His arms grew ever stronger as he rowed toward the land; with each stroke he faced them and gazed at them intently. When he drew close enough to see their faces, a faint sigh escaped his mouth, like that of the blind man when he suddenly regains the gift of sight. He felt the rapture of the drowning man, when his feet chance upon a jutting rock—for he had spied the girl that he desired, the mistress of the image that he bore on his breast, reposing on the riverbank, set as though in a halo of her peers. Everything was, as we have said, suffused with the spirit of dreams, as he steered the boat closer beside them. Finally, Djedef stood up in it, with his handsome frame in his elegant white uniform, which fitted over his body as though he were a statue of divine potency and seductive beauty. He was like a god of the Nile, revealed by a sudden parting of the sacred waves, as he continued to stare at her of the angelic face, of that visage transparent with love and temptation. Confusion gripped the peasant girl, who kept running her eyes back and forth distractedly among her young companions. Meanwhile, they continued watching her radiant face, ignoring Djedef, who they thought was just passing by. But when they saw him standing erect in his skiff, they pulled their legs out of the water and put on their sandals, in disbelief and denial.

Djedef leapt out of the boat and strode up to within an arm's length of them, addressing the one he had come for with a tender voice, "May the Lord grant you a good evening, O lovely peasant girl!"

She glared at him with pride and scorn as she said in a

voice more melodious than those of the other birds sur-rounding her, "What do you want from us, sir? Just keep going on your way!"

He looked at her reprovingly. "You don't wish to greet me?" he asked.

Furiously she turned her head—crowned with hair black as night—away from him, while the group of women called out to him, "Keep going on your way, young man. We don't speak to those we do not know!"

"Do you see it as the custom in this fine country that raised you to greet a stranger so harshly?" Djedef replied.

One of them said sharply, "What shows upon your face is infatuation, not unfamiliarity!"

"How cruelly you are treating me!"

"If you truly were a stranger, this is not a place where strangers would come. Return south to Memphis, or go north, if you wish, and say goodbye to us in peace—for we do not speak to anyone with whom we are not acquainted!"

Djedef shrugged his shoulders dismissively and said, point-ing at the gorgeous peasant girl, "My mistress knows me."

They were again seized by disbelief and looked at the lovely girl, whom they found enraged. "That is a slanderous lie!" they heard her say to him.

"Never, by the Lord's truth. I have known you for a long time, but I hadn't resolved to find you until my patience betrayed me, and I could no longer bear to miss you so."

"How can you claim that, when I have never laid eyes on you before this moment?"

"And she doesn't want to see you after this moment, either," one of her companions quipped.

Bitterly, another complained, "There's nothing uglier than when soldiers attack girls!"

But he paid them no heed. Then he said to the one from whose face he could not turn his eyes away, "The more I see you, the more my soul is filled with you."

"Liar . . . you're shameless."

"Far be it from me that I should lie—but I bear your cruel speech with love, out of respect for the lovely mouth that utters it."

"No—you're just a liar who has been rejected, looking for a crooked way in!"

"I said, far be it from me that I should lie—and here's proof."

As he spoke, he reached his hand into his breast and pulled out the picture of her face, then told her, "Would I be able to paint this picture without filling my eyes with your splendor?"

The girl glanced at the picture—and was unable to suppress a sigh of disbelief, anger, and fear. Her companions were also indignant. One of them attacked him without warning, wanting to snatch it away from him, but he put up his arm with lightning speed, grinning triumphantly. "Do you see how you occupy my imagination and my soul?" he said.

"This is vileness and depravity," she said, seething with fury.

"Why?" he challenged her. "That you so captivated me that I created your image?"

"Give me the picture," she commanded, with a sharpness not without an element of entreaty.

"I shall not part with it, so long as I live," he replied.

"I see you are one of the soldiers from the military academy," she remarked. "Beware, then—your ill manners could expose you to the harshest of punishments."

Calmly he answered, "To gaze upon you, I would expose myself to the sternest chastisement."

"How amazing that you have brought this affliction upon yourself!"

"Yes—one that is most deserving of compassion."

"What did you want to accomplish with this picture?" she demanded.

"With this picture, I wanted to cure myself of what your eyes have done to me—and now I want you to cure me of what you have done to me with this picture," he answered.

"I never dreamed that I'd ever meet a man of your insolence."

"And did I ever dream that I would surrender my mind and my heart in a fleeting instant?"

Then another girl shouted at him, "Did you run after us in order to spoil our happiness?"

Another said to him in the same tone, "You foolish, impudent young man! If you don't leave very quickly, I'll scream for help from the people nearby!"

He looked confidently into the empty space surrounding them and said quietly, "I'm not used to asking for anything, so this is painful for me."

The beautiful peasant girl shouted, "Do you want to force me to listen to you?"

"No, but I do long that your heart would soften so it would want to hear me out."

"And if you found my heart like a rock that would not soften?"

"Could that delicate breast really enfold a stone?"

"Only when it's faced by the most foolish of fools."

"And in the face of a lover's suffering?"

She stamped the earth with her foot and said violently, "Then it becomes even crueler."

"The heart of the cruelest girl is like a block of ice: if a warm breath touches it, then it melts and pours as pure water," he retorted.

"This talk that you think so refined," she replied, sarcastically, "shows that you're a phony soldier, the body of a girl hiding in military clothes. Perhaps you stole this uniform, just as you stole my image before."

Djedef's face flushed. "May the Lord indulge you," he

said. "I truly am a soldier—and I shall win your heart, as I win in every field of battle."

"What field of battle are you talking about?" she retorted in derision. "The nation has not known war since before the art of soldiery condescended to your acquaintance. You're just a soldier whose victories are awarded in the fields of peace and safety."

Increasingly embarrassed, Djedef said, "Do you not know, my beauty, that the life of a pupil in the military academy is like that of a soldier in the field? But, since you've no knowledge of such things, my heart forgives your taunting me so."

Enraged, she burst out, "Truly I deserve rebuke—for being so patient with your impertinence!"

She was about to walk away, but he blocked her path, smiling. "I wonder how I can gain your affection?" he said. "I am very unlucky. Have you ever taken a trip on the Nile in a skiff?"

Frightened of his trapping their mistress, the girls gathered around to protect her. "Let us go now, because the sunset is upon us," one of them told him.

Yet he would not let them leave. Frustrated, one of them, searching for a moment of inattention, saw her chance and leapt upon him like a lioness, clinging to his leg and biting him on the thigh. Then they all jumped upon him, holding onto his other leg and restraining him by force. He began to resist them calmly without really defending himself, but was unable to move and saw—and the sight nearly drove him mad—the lovely peasant girl running toward the end of the field like a fleeing gazelle. He called out to her begging for her help, but lost his balance and fell upon the grass, while the others still clung to him, not letting go until they were sure that their mistress had disappeared. He stood up, agitated and angry, and ran in the direction that she had gone—

yet saw nothing but emptiness. He returned, despondent, but hoping to find her by following her companions. Yet they outsmarted him, refusing to budge from their places.

"Stay or go now as you wish," one of them said mockingly.

"Perhaps, soldier boy, this is your first defeat," said another, maliciously.

"The battle is not finished yet," he answered in utter pique. "I'll follow you even if you go to Thebes."

But the one who first bit him said, "We will spend our night here."

17

The next month that he spent in the academy was the longest and cruelest of all. At first he was in great pain over his sullied honor and pride, asking himself wrathfully, "How could I have suffered such a setback? What do I lack in youth, good looks, strength, or wealth?" He would gaze a long time into the mirror and mutter, "What's wrong with me?" What, indeed, had driven the gorgeous creature away from him? What had brought down insult after insult upon him? Why had she fled from him as though he were a leper? But then his intense desire to pursue her and capture her would return, and he would wonder, if he persisted in wooing her day after day, would he be able to curb her defiance and win her heart? What girl can be cruel forever? But this came to him while he was a prisoner for a month behind those huge walls that could withstand any siege.

Despite all this, he remained under her spell, her portrait never leaving his vest; he gave it all his attention whenever he found himself alone. "Do you see who this enchanting tyrant is?" he thought to himself. "A little peasant girl? Incredible . . . and what peasant girl has such luminous, magical eyes? And where was the modesty of the peasant in her arrogance and her stubbornness? And where was the peasant's simplicity in her biting sarcasm and her resounding scorn?" If he had surprised a true peasant girl that way, perhaps she would have run away—or surrendered contentedly—but that is hardly what happened here! Could he ever forget her sitting there among her companions like a princess with her servants and ladies-in-waiting? And could he ever forget how they defended her from him, as though unto death? And would he ever forget how they stayed with him—after her flight—not running away, afraid that he would follow them to her? Instead, they resigned themselves to the cold and dark. Would they have done all those things for a peasant girl like themselves? Perhaps she was from the rural aristocracy—if only she was. Then Nafa could not taunt him again that he was likely to fall in a broken-down hut. If only he had succeeded with her, so that he could tell Nafa about it. What a pity!

Be all that as it may, the month that he imagined would never end, finally did. He left the academy as one would leave a fearful prison, and went to the house with a pent-up yearning for something other than his family. He met them with a joy not equal to theirs, and sat among them with an absent heart. Nor did he notice the stiffness and listlessness that had come over Gamurka, as he waited with an empty patience, when minutes seemed like months. Finally, he made off for the pure place of Apis where his eyes would seek out the beloved face.

This was the month of Barmuda—the air was humid and mild, taking from the cold a pinch of its freshness, and from the heat a lively breath that stirred playfulness and passion. The sky was tinted a delicate, translucent white, a pale blue gleaming beyond.

He looked tenderly at the dear spot, and asked himself, "Where is the peasant girl with the bewitching eyes?" Would she remember him? Was she still angry with him? And was his desire still so daunting for her? Could it be that his love would find an echo within her?

The empty place did not reply, the rocks were deaf to his

call—and a spirit of pessimism, longing, and solitude possessed him.

And time—first hope tempted him to believe that there was still enough for her to appear, so it passed slowly and heavily. Then despair made him imagine that she had already come and gone, and time flew like an arrow, while the sun seemed to be riding a speedy chariot racing off into the western horizon.

He kept wandering around where he saw her for the first time, peering into the green grass, longing to see the tracks of her sandals or the drag-mark of her skirt. Alas, the grass preserved no more trace of her body than had the waters retained the shape of her legs!

Does she still visit this place as she did before, or did she give up her outings to avoid seeing him? Where could she be? And how could he find her? Should he call out, but without knowing the name to call? He kept on meandering around the beloved place in confusion, his patience running out, battered back and forth by optimism and dejection. In the midst of these musings he looked up at the sky, and saw the fire of the sun going down. His eye looked upon it as though it were a human giant humbled by old age and infirmities. But then he turned his face toward the sprawling fields and saw the outline of a village. Not knowing what he was doing, he set out to reach it, and midway he met a peasant returning home after his long day's labor, and asked him about the place. The peasant answered him, staring at his uniform with respect, "It is the village of Ashar, sir." Djedef nearly showed him the picture snuggled against his breast to ask him about its mistress, but did not.

He resumed his aimless journey. Yet he found relief in the traveling that he did not find in stopping and walking around. It was as if the disappointed hope that had beguiled him on the bank of the Nile had fled into the precincts of this village and he was following its trail. It was an evening he would not forget, for he crisscrossed all the hamlet's lanes, reading the faces of those that he passed, stopping to ask at each house. As he did so, his searching look aroused curiosity, and his good looks attracted stares, with eyes locked on him from every side. Nor was it long before he found himself ambling amidst a throng of girls, boys, and older youths. The talk and clamor began to rise, while he found not a trace of the cherished object of his quest. Soon he shunned the people of the village as he left it quickly, speeding his steps toward the Nile in the gloom of his soul, and the darkness of the world.

Though grieving, his ardor burned within him, while the sense of loss tore him apart. His condition reminded him of the ordeal of Goddess Isis when she went looking for the remnants of her husband Osiris—whose body evil Seth had scattered to the winds. Mother Isis had been more fortunate than he was. If his own beloved were a phantom that one sees in dreams, then his chances of finding her would have been much stronger.

Handsome Djedef was in love, but his was an odd infatuation, one without a beloved, a passion whose agony was not from rejection or betrayal or the vagaries of time, or from people's wiles. Rather, his torment was the absence of a sweetheart altogether. She was like an errant breeze born by cyclone winds which took it to a place unknown to man. His heart was lost, not knowing a place of rest. He knew not if it was near or far, in Memphis or in the farthest parts of Nubia. How cruel were the Fates that turned his eye toward that picture that he kept next to his heart—ruthless Fates, like those spirits who take delight in the torments of men.

———

He returned to his house, where he met his brother Nafa in the garden.

"Where have you been, Djedef?" the artist asked. "You

were gone a long time—didn't you know that Kheny is in his room?"

"Kheny?" he asked, taken aback. "Is it true what you say? But I didn't find him when I came."

"He arrived in the past two hours, and he's waiting for you."

Djedef hurried to the room of the priest, whom he had not set eyes on in years. He saw him sitting as he did during the days gone by, book in hand. When Kheny saw him he stood up and said to him with joy, "Djedef! How are you, O gallant officer!"

They clasped each other around the neck for a long while, as Kheny kissed his cheeks and blessed him in the name of the Lord Ptah. Then he said, "How fleetly the years pass, O Djedef! Your face is still as handsome as ever . . . but you have grown into something quite spectacular. To me you look like those intrepid soldiers that the king blesses at the end of great battles, and whose heroism he immortalizes on the walls of the temples. My dear Djedef, how happy I am to see you after all these long years!"

Filled with joy, Djedef said, "I too am very happy, my dear brother. My God, you've turned out the faithful image of the men of the priesthood, in the leanness of your body, the dignity of your presence, and the sharpness of your expression. Have you finished your studies, my dear Kheny?"

Kheny smiled as he sat, clearing a space for Djedef next to him.

"The priest never stops learning, for there is no end to knowledge," he expounded. "Kagemni taught, 'The learned man seeks knowledge from the cradle to the grave—yet he dies an ignorant man.' Nonetheless, I have finished the first stage of study."

"And how was your life in the temple?"

Kheny turned dreamy eyes upon him. "Oh how long it has been!" he replied. "It's as though I were listening to you ten years ago, when you would hurl a question at me—do you remember, Djedef? You shouldn't be surprised, for a priest's life is spent between question and answer—or between a question and the attempt to answer it. The question is the summary of the spiritual life. Pardon me, Djedef, but what interests you about life in the temples? Not all of what is known is uttered. Suffice it that you be aware it is a life of inner struggle and purity. They habituate us to making the body pure and obedient to our will, then they teach us the divine knowledge. For where does the good seed grow except in the good soil?"

"And what are you busying yourself with, dear brother?" asked Djedef.

"I shall soon work as a servant of the sacrifices to Lord Ptah, exalted be His name. I have won the sympathy of the high priest, who has predicted that it will not be ten years before I am elected one of the ten judges of Memphis."

"I believe that His Holiness's prophecy will come true before then," Djedef said with passion. "You are a great man, my brother."

Kheny grinned in his quiet way. "I thank you, dear Djedef. And now, tell me, are you reading anything useful?"

Djedef laughed. "If that's how you count military strategy, or the history of the Egyptian army, then I'm reading something useful!"

Then Kheny inquired empathetically, "Wisdom, O Djedef! You were listening to the words of the sages with zeal in this very place, but ten years ago!"

"The truth is that you planted the love of wisdom in my heart," Djedef said. "But my life in the military leaves me little free time for the reading I crave. Be that as it may, the distance between myself and liberation has been shortened."

Disturbed, Kheny said, "The virtuous mind never dismisses wisdom even for a day, just as the healthy stomach does not renounce food for a day. You should make up for what you have already lost, O Djedef. The virtue of the science of war is that it trains the soldier to serve his homeland and his sovereign with his might, though his soul does not benefit at all. And the soldier who is ignorant of wisdom is like the faithful beast—nothing more. Perhaps he would do well under an iron hand, but if left to his own devices, he is unable to help himself, and can help only others instead. The gods have distinguished him from the animals by giving him a soul, and if the soul isn't nourished by wisdom then it sinks to the level of the lesser creatures. Don't neglect this, O Djedef, for I feel from the depths of my heart that your spirit is lofty, and I read on your handsome forehead splendid lines of majesty and glory, may the Lord bless your comings and your goings."

The conversation flowed between them sweetly and agreeably, closing with the subject of Nafa's marriage. Kheny learned of it for the first time from Djedef, calling down blessings on the husband and the wife. Then a thought occurred to Djedef and he asked, "Kheny, won't you marry?"

"Why not, Djedef?" the priest said to the young man. "The clergyman cannot remain sure of his own wisdom if he does not marry. Can mortal man ascend to heaven with a soul still yearning for the earth? The virtue of marriage is that it takes care of one's lust and so purifies the body."

———

Djedef left his brother's chamber at midnight, and repaired to his own room. He had started to remove his robe while recalling his talk with the priest, when sorrow assailed him as he remembered his day, and the frustration it had brought him. But just before dropping onto his bed he heard a light tapping, and he bid the person knocking to come in.

Zaya entered, her face distressed.

"Did I awake you?" she asked him.

"No, Mama, I hadn't gone to sleep yet," he said, feeling afraid. "Is everything alright?"

The woman hesitated, trying to speak, but her tongue would not obey. She gestured for him to follow her, and he did so apprehensively until she halted at her bedroom. She pointed at the floor—and Djedef saw Gamurka sprawled out as though wounded by a fatal shaft. He could not control himself as he cried out in alarm, "Gamurka . . . Gamurka . . . what's wrong with him, Mama?"

With a choking voice, the woman said, "Have courage, Djedef, have courage."

His heart torn out of his chest, the soldier knelt by the dear dog, which did not greet him as normal by leaping about with joy. He stroked his body but Gamurka did not stir.

"Mama, what's the matter with him?" he asked again.

"Be brave, Djedef, for he is dying."

The fearsome word horrified Djedef. "How did this happen?" he said in a protesting tone. "He came to see me this morning, the way he always does."

"He wasn't like he always was, my dear. Even though his love for you obliterated his pain at the time, he's now very old, Djedef, and the final feebleness has been clear in him these last few days."

Djedef's pain intensified; he turned to his faithful friend and whispered into his ear in deepest grief, "Gamurka . . . don't you hear me? Gamurka!"

The trusty dog lifted his head with difficulty, looking at his master with unseeing eyes, as though he was bidding the final goodbye. Then he returned to his heavy sleep, and began to moan hoarsely, as Djedef called to him time and again, but without any response at all. He sensed that the force of death was gathering around his loyal comrade, watching as he opened and closed his mouth, panting heavily. He crouched helplessly as Gamurka shuddered weakly just once, before journeying quietly into Eternity. He called out to him from the depths of his heart, "Gamurka," but the plea was futile. For the first time since becoming a soldier, the tears flowed from his eyes as he wept in farewell for the companion of his childhood, the dear friend of his boyhood, and the comrade of his youth.

His mother lifted him up before her and dried his tears with her lips, then sat him down next to her on her bed, consoling him with tender words—but he did not hear. Nor did he open his mouth all that night except when he told her, "Mama, I want to embalm him and lay him in a sarcophagus. Then I want to put him in the spot in the garden where he and I used to play—until he's moved into my tomb when the Lord calls me to Him."

And so ended that tragic day.

18

Djedef's sixth and final year in the war college had finished. The school held its traditional annual tournament in which the graduates contended with each other before being assigned to the various branches of the army. A vivid liveliness dawned that day on the mighty academy, its walls adorned with the standards of the military divisions, the air resounding with the rousing strains of music.

The doors opened to receive the invitees, both men and women, whose masses came from the families of the army officers and commanders, as well as the graduates and high officials.

After midday, there came the great men of state, led by the priests and ministers. At their head were His Holiness Hemiunu, the Military High Commander under Arbu, plus many of the other leading civil servants, scribes, and artists. They all assembled there in order to receive His Royal Highness Prince Khafra, the heir apparent, whom His Majesty the King had appointed to preside over the celebration in his name.

When the time of the prince's arrival drew nigh, the elite men of office hastened to the academy's gateway and stood waiting amidst lines of soldiers. Before long there appeared in the broad, level square in front of the school the crown prince's procession, led by a troop of chariots from the Great House Guards. The music played in salute as the masses stood in tribute, their cheers rising for Khufu and the crown prince.

When Khafra's retinue reached the building's entrance, the academy's director approached, bearing in his hands a silken cushion stuffed with ostrich feathers upon which His Royal Highness would rest his feet. With Khafra came his sister, Her Royal Highness Princess Meresankh, as well as his brothers, the princes Baufra, Hordjedef, Horsadef, Kawab, Sedjedef, Khufukhaf, Hata, and Meryb.

The notables bowed before the crown prince, who walked with a hardened face and square build that the maturity of age made seem even harsher and more vainglorious. As he took his seat in the center, the princess and the other princes sat at his right, while to his left were Hemiunu, the ministers, the commanders, and the chief civil officials. After the prince's arrival, the cheering quieted down as the guests were seated, and the festivities began. The horn sounded, the music was played, and from the direction of the barracks there appeared a group of graduating officers marching four abreast, headed by the commander of the trainees, holding the school's standard. For the first time they were dressed in officers' uniform with its green shirt, loincloth, and leopard-skin cape.

When they reached a point parallel to the throne upon which His Royal Highness reposed, they drew out their swords and raised them with arms outstretched like pillars, their tips pointed skyward, offering their salute. Khafra, standing, returned it.

The great competition commenced with a horse race. The officers mounted colorfully adorned steeds and lined up in formation. When the horn sounded, they plunged forward like arrows shot from giant bows, the legs of the chargers shaking the ground like a powerful earthquake. Their pace was so fast that the onlookers almost lost sight of them, while the brave riders clung to them as though nailed to their backs. At first there was a single row, then the violent pace began to pull them apart. Suddenly, one horseman bolted free of the others as though riding a mad wind, beating them back to the starting place. The trainer announced the name of this rider—"Djedef son of Bisharu"—as the winner. If, amidst the thunderous applause, he had been able to hear his father cheering, "Go, son of Bisharu!" he would not have been able to control his laughter.

A short time later, the chariot race began. The officers mounted their vehicles and waited in formation. Then the horn blew as they burst out like giants, sending terror out before them, leaving a roar behind them like the breaking of boulders and the sundering of mountains. They swayed in their vehicles without wavering, like firmly rooted palm trunks buffeted by winds determined to upend them—winds that were forced to give up in wailing frustration.

Suddenly there raced out from among them a rider who sped past them all with preternatural power, who moved so quickly that they seemed to be standing still. He was headed for victory right until the end, when the trainer again announced the name of the winner—"Djedef son of Bisharu." Again, the cheers rose for him, and this time the clapping was even stronger.

Next the crier proclaimed that it was time for the steeplechase. Once more the officers mounted their horses, as wooden benches, whose height gradually increased one after another, were set up in the midst of the long field. With the blast of the horn, the horses bounded forward abruptly, flying over the first obstacle like attacking eagles. They leapt over the second like the waves of a ferocious waterfall, clear victory seeming to crown them as they progressed. But fortune betrayed most of them. The horses of some could not hear their commands; others stumbled amidst piteous cries. Only one horseman cleared all the hurdles as though he were an inexorable Fate, the embodiment of conquest. The crier called out his name, "Djedef son of Bisharu," to the crowd's huge praise and applause.

Victory was his ally in all of the trials. He hit the target most accurately with lances and in archery. He humbled all comers with swords and with axes. The gods made his an absolute triumph. He was the hero of that day without any equal, the academy's prodigy without any peer, winning a place of wonder and appreciation in every heart there.

The winners were expected to approach the heir apparent so that he might congratulate them on their abilities. That day, Djedef went alone to offer the prince the military salute, and the heir apparent put his hand in his, saying, "I congratulate you, fearless Officer: first, for your superiority over all in the field; and second, for my selecting you to be an officer in my special guard."

The young man's face was flooded with joy as he saluted the prince and returned to his place. Along the way he heard the crier announce to those in attendance that the prince had congratulated him and had chosen him to be a member of his guard. His heart fluttered as he thought of his family's excitement—Bisharu, Zaya, Kheny, and Nafa—who were listening to the crier's speech, and who were experiencing the same indescribable delirium.

After that, the troop of new officers marched up to the crown prince's throne so that he might address them, saying in his gruff voice: "O valiant officers, I hereby declare my full satisfaction with your courage, your talent, your enthusiasm, and your noble soldierly character. I hope that you will continue to be, like your brethren who have come before you, an ensign of glory for your homeland and for Pharaoh, Lord of the Two Lands."

The soldiers cheered for the homeland and for Pharaoh. Thence came the announcement that the celebration was finished. As the invited guests departed, the heir apparent left the academy and his official procession returned to the royal palace.

During all this, Djedef was in a kind of daze that insulated him from what was going on around him. This was not the euphoria of victory—rather, it was a more serious and engrossing concern. For while he was listening to the prince's speech with his classmates, his eyes drifted from the speaker, only to find them settling on Princess Meresankh. Thunderstruck, he nearly fell on his face. By the gods in heaven, what did he see but the face of the peasant girl whose portrait he carried next to his heart! He wanted to look at it longer, but he feared that would cause a scandal, so he stared straight ahead without paying attention to anything. And when the gala ended and he recovered from his sudden surprise, he made his way back to the barracks like one touched by madness.

Could it be that his beautiful farmer's daughter is really Her Royal Highness Princess Meresankh? That seemed beyond belief—impossible even to imagine!

On the other hand, could one easily accept that there existed two faces with this same bewitching beauty? And had he forgotten the arrogance that the one in the picture showed him—a behavior not found among peasant girls? Yet all of these things together could not support this bizarre conjecture: if only he could carry out further inquiries in the features of her face!

And what, then, if she is the princess? Something immense had come to him whose consequences he could not predict. At this he lost his self-control and laughed with bitter derision. "How fantastic!" he told himself. "Djedef son of Bisharu is in love with the princess, Meresankh!" Then he gazed at the picture forlornly for quite a long time.

"Are you truly the majestic princess?" he demanded of her image. "Be a simple peasant girl—for a peasant girl lost is nearer to the heart than a princess found."

19

Djedef made ready to leave Bisharu's palace as an independent man for the first time. And this time he would leave behind him sadness mixed with admiration and pride, as Zaya kissed him until she drenched his cheeks with her tears. Kheny, too, blessed him in farewell: the priest himself had started preparing to depart their home for the temple. Meanwhile, Nafa gripped his hand warmly, saying, "The passing days will prove my prophecy true, O Djedef." And a new member of Bisharu's family likewise bid him goodbye—this was Mana, daughter of Kamadi and wife of Nafa. As for old Bisharu, he put his coarse hand on the soldier's shoulder and told him with conceit, "I am happy, Djedef, that you are taking your first steps on the path of your great father." Nor did Djedef forget to lay a lotus blossom on Gamurka's grave before taking leave of his house on the way to the palace of His Royal Pharaonic Highness, Prince Khafra.

By fortunate coincidence, one of his comrades in the prince's barracks was an old childhood friend, a decent, frank-spoken, warmhearted boy. His companion of yore, whose name was Sennefer, rejoiced at his arrival, receiving him warmly.

"Are you always on my trail?" he asked him, teasingly.

"So long as you're on the road to glory," Djedef answered, grinning.

"Yours is the glory, Djedef. I once was champion of the chariot race, but as for you, there's never been a soldier like yourself: I congratulate you from my deepest heart."

Djedef thanked him, and in the evening, Sennefer drew a flask of Maryut wine from his robe along with two silver goblets, saying, "I've grown accustomed to drinking a glass of this before going to sleep; a very beneficial ritual. Do you ever drink?"

"I drink beer—but why would I drink wine?"

Sennefer burst out laughing. "Drink!" he said. "Wine is the warrior's medicine."

Then suddenly, he said to him seriously, "O brother Djedef, you have accepted an arduous life!"

Djedef smiled and said, somewhat disdainfully, "I am quite used to the soldier's life."

"All of us are used to military life. But His Royal Highness is something else entirely," Sennefer confided.

Surprise showed on Djedef's face. "What do you mean?" he asked.

"I'm counseling you, brother, on the obvious truth of the matter—and to warn you," Sennefer said. "Serving the prince is a hardship like no other."

"How is that?" asked Djedef.

"His Highness is extremely cruel, with a heart of stone, or even harder," he confided. "A mistake to him is a deliberate offense," Sennefer explained, "and a deliberate offense, to him, is a crime that cannot be forgiven. Egypt will find in him a strict ruler who does not treat a wound with balsam, as His Majesty his father sometimes does. Rather, he would not hesitate to cut off the worthless limb should it hinder him."

"The firm monarch needs a bit of cruelty," said Djedef.

"A bit of cruelty, yes—but not cruelty in all things," Sennefer continued. "You'll see everything for yourself in due course. Yet there hardly comes a day when a number of punishments aren't issued, some against the servants, some against the soldiers, some for the lower ranks, and perhaps some for the officers. And as time goes by, he only gets nastier—more boastful and crude, in fact."

"Usually, a man's nature softens as the years advance—this is what Kagemni says."

Sennefer laughed loudly as he said, "'It is not becoming for an officer to quote the sayings of the wise.' That is what His Highness says! His Highness's life deviates from Kagemni's description. Why? Because he's forty years old. A crown prince who's forty—think of it!"

The young man looked at him quizzically, as Sennefer went on talking in a low voice. "One wants heirs apparent to come to power young, for if the Fates are awful to them, then they are awful to everyone else!" he opined.

"Isn't His Highness married?"

"And he has both boys and girls," answered Sennefer.

"Then the throne is secure for his progeny."

"This does nothing to relieve his chagrin . . . it's not what the prince fears."

"What does he fear, then? His brothers uphold the laws of the kingdom honestly."

"There's no doubt about that," said Sennefer. "Perhaps they lack ambition because their mothers are just concubines in the harem—and Her Majesty the Queen gave birth only to the crown prince and his sister, Meresankh. The throne rightfully belongs to those two before anyone else. But what worries the prince is . . . the vigorous health of His Majesty the King!"

"Pharaoh is idolized by all Egypt," said Djedef.

"There's no argument there," the officer said. "But I imagine that I can see the lusts lodged deep in people's souls that the conscience does not allow to emerge. God forbid that a traitor be found in Egypt. No, brother . . . and now, what's your opinion of the Maryut wine? I'm Theban, but I'm not prejudiced."

"What you served me was fine," Djedef replied.

This was enough chatter for Sennefer, who went off to sleep. But Djedef's cheek never touched his pillow, because his friend's mention of Meresankh had stirred his anguish and his burning love, just as food thrown on the water's surface excites the fish's hunger. Restive and disturbed, he spent the long, black night exchanging secrets with his sorrowing heart.

20

Within the heir apparent's palace, Djedef felt deep inside that he was close to an obscure secret. No doubt, he dwelt on the horizon where it would arise—and, inevitably, one of its blazing rays would someday illuminate it. Meanwhile, he waited in hope, in fear, and in rapture.

One late afternoon, he patrolled the palace meadows that overlooked the Nile, as the sun of the month of Hatur poured forth a joyous light recalling the days of his youthful prime and splendor. Making his rounds, he saw a royal ship lying in anchor at the garden's staircase—and none of the chamberlains were there to greet it. So he hurried—as duty obliged—to receive the honored messenger, and stood facing the ship like a striking statue.

He saw a divine, glorious vision hidden in the robe of a king's daughter. With pharaonic grandeur and ethereal grace, she came down from the ship to ascend the staircase. So ethereal was she, in fact, it seemed as though her weight was pulled upward, not downward. Djedef was looking at Her Royal Highness Princess Meresankh!

He drew out his long sword and gave a military salute, as the princess passed by him like a ravishing dream. And just as quickly, she departed the twisting paths of the garden.

How could this not be her?

Sight can be deceived, and so can hearing, but the heart

never is—and if this wasn't her, then his heart would not beat so intensely that it was almost torn to pieces. And why else would it leave him in ecstasy like a staggering drunk? Yet her mind seemed neither to sense or to recall him—and hadn't something happened between them that would merit remembrance? Could she so quickly forget so strange an encounter? Or could she be just snobbishly pretending not to know him?

And what good would it do him, whether she remembered him or not? What is the difference between the princess being the girl in the picture, or someone else who resembles her? For his heart beats so hard only for the love of this lovely painting, and shall continue to do so, whether she resides in the body of the princess from the Great House of Pharaoh, or in that of the peasant girl from the villages around Memphis. And he shall remain in despair of her in either case, for there is no alternative to love—just as there is none to its denial.

He set his gaze toward the trees, and saw the birds drawn by their branches, continually warbling in song, their appearance announcing their joy from passionate love and affection. He felt a sentiment for them that he had not known before. He envied that they could cavort without cost, that they could love without torment, and that their natures transcended all doubts and illusions. He looked at his own colored uniform, his cocky headdress, and his sword, and felt insignificant: he had an urge to laugh at himself with snickering bitterness.

He had mastered archery and horseback riding, and excelled in hand-to-hand combat, achieving all that to which a youth aspires—yet he knew not how to make himself happy! Nafa was more fortunate because he had married Mana of the long, graceful neck and honey-colored eyes. And Kheny would wed in quiet simplicity, because he views marriage as a religious obligation. As for Djedef, he had to keep hidden within his breast a secret, despairing love, which withered his heart the way that the denial of Nile water and sun withers the leafy tree.

He remained rooted where he stood, longing to see her yet another time. To him, this visit seemed clearly unofficial, for had it been known by all in the palace, they would have received her in a manner appropriate to her station in the royal family. Therefore it was certainly possible that she would return to the boat by herself. His thinking turned out to be correct, for the princess reappeared alone after His Royal Highness had bid her goodbye at the palace entrance.

Djedef was at his place by the garden's staircase, in attendant readiness, until—when she passed by in front of him—he drew out his sword in salute. Suddenly Meresankh stopped and turned toward him with highborn hauteur, inquiring bitingly, "Do you know your duties, Officer?"

"Yes, your Highness," he blurted, shaken as though by an earthquake.

"Do your duties include kidnapping maidens other than in time of war?"

As embarrassment seized him, she continued staring cruelly at him for a moment, then said, "Is it a soldier's duty to act treacherously?"

Unable to bear the pain, he told her, "O my mistress, the brave soldier never behaves treacherously."

At this, she asked him mockingly, "Then what would you say to one who skulks in waiting behind the trees for virtuous maidens, and paints them on the sly?"

Then her tone changed. "You should know that I want that picture," she demanded sternly.

Djedef obeyed, as he was accustomed to obey. He put his hand into his breast, pulling the painting out of its deep hiding place, and presented it to the princess.

She had not been expecting this. Surprise flashed on her face, in spite of her pride—but she soon regained her grip on herself as she stretched forth her soft-skinned hand and snatched the image from him.

Then she processed back to her ship, enveloped in majesty and grandeur.

Djedef's life in the prince's palace went on with nothing novel on the horizon, until one day he discovered a new source of pain.

On that day, His Highness Prince Khafra went out in his most exalted ceremonial uniform, preceded by a squadron of guards, among them Djedef's friend Sennefer. The prince returned toward the evening, and Sennefer came back to his chamber at the same time that Djedef did after fulfilling his duty, both as a guard and as inspector of the guards. Of course, it would have been natural to ask his friend what had prompted the prince to go out in a manner reserved usually for the great feasts. But he knew from experience that Sennefer was the sort who could not keep a secret. And in fact, Sennefer had only relaxed briefly when he said, while pulling on his nightshirt, "Do you know where we went today?"

"No" said Djedef, calmly.

"His Highness Prince Ipuwer, governor of Arsina Nome," Sennefer said, weightily, "went to Memphis today—where he was received by the heir apparent!"

"Isn't His Highness the son of His Majesty the King's maternal uncle?"

"Yes," answered Sennefer, "and it is said that His Highness came bearing a report on the tribes of Sinai—there have been many more incidents lately involving them in the lands of the Eastern Delta."

"Then His Highness was a herald of war?"

"True enough, Djedef," replied Sennefer. "And what I've learned is that for a long time, the crown prince has leaned toward taming the tribes of Sinai, and Commander Arbu supports his view. Yet Pharaoh preferred to be patient until the country's forces were ready, after the huge effort expended in construction, especially in building the king's pyramid. After waiting for a time, the prince asked for the fulfillment of what his father had promised. But it's said that His Majesty the King is preoccupied these days in writing his great book, which he wants to make the greatest guide in both religious and worldly affairs for the Egyptians. So, as the king didn't seem prepared to think seriously about the question of war, Prince Khafra turned to his relative Prince Ipuwer. He agreed that he would meet with him himself to advise the king on the facts of the tribes' insolence and their disdain for the government's authority, and of the consequences should this situation continue. Therefore, it seems likely that with the prince's coming a division of the army will be marching northeast in the very near future."

Silence reigned for a moment, then Sennefer, driven by his love of chatter, resumed, "His Majesty the King threw a banquet for the prince, attended by all the members of the royal family. At their head were Pharaoh and the princesses."

Djedef's heart pounded at the mention of the princesses—and especially of the enchanting princess with all her magnificent beauty and pride. He sighed, without realizing that the sound had attracted Sennefer's ears. The young man looked at him in reproach and said, "By the truth of Ptah, you aren't paying attention when I speak!"

Dismayed, Djedef said, "How can you claim that?"

"Because you sighed like one who is unable to think while his mind has gone off to his sweetheart."

The pounding of Djedef's heart worsened. He tried to

speak, but Sennefer did not let him, as, laughing loudly, he said with interest, "Who is she? Come on, who is she, Djedef? Ah . . . you're giving me a look of denial. I won't press you now, because I will know her one day, when she's the mother of your children. What memories! Do you know, O Djedef, that I sighed the same way in this same room two years ago, and spent nights deluding myself with fantasies and dreams? And the next year she became my dear wife— today she is the mother of my son, Fana. What a room this is, so charged with passion! But why don't you tell me who she is?"

Djedef replied, with grief-edged sharpness, "You're deluded, Sennefer!"

"Deluded, am I? Youth, good looks, and strength—and already all dull and dried up? Impossible."

"Sennefer—it's true."

"As you wish, O Djedef—I won't insist that you answer the question. But, while we're on the subject of romance, I'll tell you that I heard whispers circulating in the corridors of Pharaoh's palace, which hint at other reasons for Prince Ipuwer's visit than the war I mentioned."

"What do you mean?"

"They say that the prince will be given a chance to see the youngest of the princesses up close—and she is of proverbial beauty. Perhaps there the people of Egypt will soon hear the news of the engagement of Prince Ipuwer to Princess Mere-sankh."

This time Djedef felt extremely weak, but he took control of himself, stifled his emotions, and met the blow with stunning forbearance. His face gave nothing away of the battle raging within him, securing him from the danger of his friend's sharp eyes and his painful, gossipy tongue. He was wary of commenting at all on what Sennefer had said, or to ask him for more details or clarifications, for fear that he would be given away by the tone of his voice. So he maintained a heavy, terror-stricken silence, like a huge mountain weighing over the mouth of a volcano.

Sennefer, unaware of what was happening to his companion, threw himself down on his bed. Yawning, he continued his gossip. "Princess Meresankh is a great beauty," he ventured. "Have you ever seen her? She's the loveliest of the princesses. And, like her brother the crown prince, she's terrifically arrogant, with a will of iron. They say Pharaoh loves her like no one else. The price for her looks will be very high—no doubt about that. Beauty certainly turns men's heads. . . ."

Sennefer yawned again, then closed his eyes. Djedef stared at him in the feeble lamplight with eyes clouded by misery. When he was sure that Sennefer had surrendered to sleep, he moaned to himself in torment. Shunning his bed and feeling an intense unrest, he grew weary, and tiptoed out of the room. The air was moist, with a chilling breeze, and the night black as pitch. In the darkness, the date palms looked like slumbering ghosts, or souls whose tortures stretched through eternity.

After a few days, all in the palace knew that His Highness the Crown Prince had invited Prince Ipuwer, along with Her Highness Princess Meresankh, plus various other princes and companions, on a hunt in the Eastern Desert.

On the morning of the appointed day came Princess Meresankh. Her face was a nimbus of splendor, lighting up hearts and flooding them with joy. Just behind her came His Highness Ipuwer accompanied by his retinue. Thirty-five years old and powerfully built, his whole appearance proclaimed his nobility, honor, and courage.

The chief chamberlain himself had overseen the preparations for the hunting party, which he had provisioned with all necessary water, stores, weapons, and netting. The chief of the guard picked a hundred soldiers from his force to escort the expedition, putting ten officers—among them Djedef—in command over them. Aside from all these there were also the servants, aides, and hunters. Then, at the heir apparent's arrival in the palace garden, the great caravan began to move. At its head was a troop of horsemen well acquainted with the route for the hunt, while behind them came His Pharaonic Highness Prince Khafra, the alluring Princess Meresankh at his right, Prince Ipuwer at his left. Surrounding them was a cluster of nobles and princes. Following this magnificent defile came a wagon bearing water, and another holding the stores, cooking utensils, and tents, while trailing them came the third, fourth, and fifth wagons, carrying the hunting tackle, bows, and arrows. All of them proceeded between two lines of mounted horsemen, as the rest of the chariots from the guard troop, headed by its officers, Djedef among them, brought up the rear. The caravan ambled eastward, leaving behind the crowded city and the sacred Nile. As it headed into the desert, nothing seemed to surround them but the daunting horizon. No matter how long one marched, its expanse—stretching ever onward—seemed to retreat further, like one's shadow, with each step taken.

The morning was dewy, and as the sun rose, it covered the badlands with a carpet of light. Yet the cool breeze rendered the harsh sun harmless, as they sheltered among its rays like lion cubs gripped by their mother's fangs.

And so the caravan progressed, following the guides.

In the distance, Djedef could see the young princess who tyrannized his soul, and who had caused him to fall tortuously in love. Her brightly plumed horse stretched its back proudly as she swayed in her saddle like a tender branch. Her expression was haughty, except when she looked at her brother occasionally to say something to him, or to listen to him speaking. Then her left profile was like the image of the goddess Isis on temple walls. And when the virile Prince Ipuwer leaned toward her with his strong form, talking to her and smiling, she spoke and smiled back to him. This was the first time that Djedef saw she who had such arrogance be so generous with her smile, as though she were the sky of Egypt—clear, lovely, beautiful, and rare to rain.

And for the first time, the poison of jealousy crept into his heart, as he threw the happy Ipuwer a fiery look—that fortunate prince who had come as a messenger of strife, but on his way was transformed into the prophet of peace and love. Djedef's heart suffered a biting irritability that his pure soul had never before known, and he kept chiding himself in agitation and anger.

Could it really be that he had fallen in love and was pining away in the chill of despair, while losing the world altogether? Is it reasonable that one who endures the utmost fires of love, who feels such passionate desire, should pace but a horse's jump away from the one that he craves? What, then, is the value of life? And of what value are the hopes that have given him such strength and durability? How his life resembled a succulent rose, whose blossoms have not been savored, overwhelmed by a violent summer wind that has plucked it from its gentle stem, and buried it in the burning sands of the desert.

Who then is this slave that they call obedience? And who is this tyrant whose name is duty? What is princely authority, and what is bondage? How can these terms break down his heart and toss it into the wind of resignation? Why does he not pull out his sword and pounce with his swift steed on this cruel, haughty female? Why, with his power and skill, does he not carry her away, disappearing with her into the depths of the desert? Then he could say to her, "Look at me: I am the strong man and you are the weak woman. Lose that frown that the habits of the pharaonic palace have drawn on your face. Lower that chin that the customs of sovereign authority have raised so high. Get rid of that arrogant gaze that you have grown used to leveling at those kneeling before you, and come kneel before me. If you want love, I will welcome you with love—and if you do not, you will meet only disdain."

What drivel this is, like the boiling of a kettle, its lid shut tight! Mere suppressed anger, without any effect! The caravan moves on, and here comes passion, playing with people's hearts. Figures sway to its magic, and lips become languid. Here are the vast deserts that bear witness in eternal silence—and what deserts these are! He contemplated the wasteland for quite a long while, then fear rescued him from his painful dreams. It drained him of all sense of awe and majesty—even though the caravan was like no more than a fistful of water in a shoreless sea. Does the circling kite want to be seen by the clutch of little chicks? What is his love, anyway? And what are his agonies to anyone else? Who can feel them, in that infinite space, and how one's cry is lost in that endless universe! What does Djedef himself matter—and who can care about his love?

The sudden snorting of his horse alerted him to his surroundings. The caravan had been advancing steadily until its forward part reached the place called Rayyan, and they halted for rest. This was among the most favorable spots in the desert for hunting, with Mt. Seth stretching by it north to south, a refuge for the various kinds of animals that hunters seek. From the mountain's slope to what bordered it in the east, two great hills extended, enclosing a large patch of desert, then they narrowed as they stretched eastward. Ultimately, only twenty arm lengths separate them in a very rare and special place, naturally perfect for hunting and the chase.

The men began to feel tired, so the servants and soldiers rushed to put up the tents. Meanwhile, others were absorbed in organizing the cooking utensils and fuel for the fire as the work proceeded with a lively purpose. Indeed, in scarcely a few minutes a complete military camp was formed, the horses tethered, and a space cleared for the cooking fire. The guards took up their positions as the princes headed toward the grand tent raised on wooden pegs inlaid with pure gold. The princes rested for an hour, until, refreshed, they set out for the chase.

The servants set up a great hunting net near the narrowest point between the two adjoining hills. The soldiers scattered along the triangle drawn by Mt. Seth and these two smaller promontories. Others crossed onto the slope of the mountain to stampede the placid animals, while the princes mounted their horses, inspected their weapons, then spread out across the spacious plain, ready for action.

Princess Meresankh, on her elegantly trimmed steed, remained in front of the great tent to observe the expected struggle, seen time after time between men and beasts. She watched the movements of the princes with enormous interest. Evidently, she found the hunting to be slow, for in an audible voice she asked the officers that stood at the rear, without turning toward them, "What's wrong with me that I don't see any game?"

A voice she knew well answered, "The soldiers have gone off to beat the animals from the bush." It continued, "Soon, Your Highness, you should see them coming down the slope of the mountain, howling, lowing, and roaring."

She looked far off at the slope of Mt. Seth. The officer's claim proved true, for it was not long before she saw groups of gazelles, rabbits, and stags racing downhill in their differing gaits, ignorant of what the Fates had hidden from them. As they fled, the mounted princes drove them on. Then each one of them bolted after his particular prey, and the battle began. The hunters pursued the beasts in order to drive them toward the net that awaited them, its maw open wide.

Altogether, Prince Khafra was the most skilled hunter in the party. All had noticed his nimbleness and athletic trimness, his complete mastery over his horse, and his superb handling of its movements, as well as his ability to communicate with beasts, to press them hard, and to push them forward to the destination he desired. He had never failed in the chase, and nor in his aim, and had worn even his dogs to exhaustion in pursuit of his numerous victims.

Prince Ipuwer likewise displayed a rare proficiency, stirring wonder with the speed of his onslaught, the accuracy of his aim, and his physical adroitness—he was an equestrian without equal.

The princes continued in their violent diversion as time ran unnoticeably by, and the hunt almost ended in unadulterated enjoyment—if an incident hadn't occurred that nearly spoiled it entirely. Prince Khafra was chasing a fleeing gazelle below the mountain's slope: when passing a tall rise, he found his way blocked by an enormous lion, its fangs bared. Many soldiers cried out to him in warning, but—ever stalwart—he put his hand on his spear to pull it from its sheath. The lion did not wait, however, but instead made a great leap and struck Khafra's horse on the face with his massive paw. Immediately, the stallion's feet grew heavy and he stumbled about like a drunk about to fall down. As he did so, the lion crouched, preparing to bound forward again even more fiercely than before. Events were unfolding rapidly, when the prince, wielding his spear, was able to aim and hurl it at the lion—which was in midleap—with terrific force. But at that moment his horse fell dead from the lion's first blow, and the spear flew wide of its mark, sparing the big cat. The prince fell on his back, far from any weapon, at the mercy of his feline foe.

As this was happening, the princes, soldiers, and officers were urging their mounts onward toward the threatened heir apparent, each one willing to give up his own life to save him. Djedef was flying on his horse like a bird through the air, quickly covering the distance that separated him from the prince, beating the others to him, arriving just as the lion made his fatal leap. Not wasting a moment, he drew out his long spear, and, grasping it with both hands, leapt from the back of his galloping horse with immense speed, falling like a flaming meteor on the raging lion. Planting his lance in the monster's mouth, he pierced it through to the sandy ground, where the lion, transfixed, could not reach him with his claws. The other princes and soldiers then caught up with them and—circling the heir apparent—fired arrows at the dying beast until it expired. Princess Mere-sankh appeared on her own stallion, terrified, her comely face clothed with horror and fear. Seeing her brother standing healthy and in one piece, she came down from her horse, ran to him and embraced him around his neck, exclaiming in heartfelt gratitude, "Praise be to the merciful Lord Ptah!"

The princes approached the heir apparent and congratulated him on his survival: they all prayed together to the Lord Ptah in profoundest thanks.

Prince Khafra looked at his slain steed with obvious regret, then walked up to the body of the lion that had nearly furnished his demise: he looked at it, arrows covering it like the fur of a hedgehog. From there he looked at the horseman standing to its right like a handsome statue. Suddenly he remembered him—the outstanding man whom he had chosen to be an officer in his personal guards. The gods, it seemed, had selected him for his role at this nerve-wracking moment, and the prince felt astonishment and gratitude toward him. He drew close to him, put his hand on his shoulder and said, "O courageous officer, you have saved me from certain death. I will repay you for your incomparable heroism with an appropriate reward."

Prince Ipuwer also came up to Djedef, whose intrepid actions had shaken him. He pumped his hand vigorously as he said, "O valorous soldier, you have rendered to your country and your king services over and above any example of appreciation."

They all returned to the camp, a heavy silence looming over them, their spirits dissipated in the numbness that follows escape from an unexpected peril. On the way back, one of the men of Prince Ipuwer's retinue said to him, "The gods would not have been pleased to torment the heart of the old king. He has locked his lofty self away in his dreary burial chamber, where he is writing for his people—all of whom love him—his thesis on survival of evil and illness. After all, how else can one repay good deeds but with more good deeds?"

The exalted gentlemen took their ease, after which they were presented with a banquet. After they had dined, the crown prince ordered the servants to distribute goblets of red Maryut wine to the soldiers in celebration of his survival. The soldiers imbibed it and prayed again in thanks to their god. Then they all sang Pharaoh's anthem with voices like the rumble of thunder reverberating through the expanse of desert. They kept this up for a while, then prepared themselves for departure. The tents were struck, the baggage and the hunting equipment packed up, and the caravan departed in the same manner that it came—except that the crown prince ordered the officer Djedef to ride in his company. He announced his wish to make Djedef one of his closest companions.

The doughty lad's heart fluttered with the rapture of joy and glory, for none enjoyed this magnificent honor except the princes and the prominent men of state. He felt an indescribable happiness in riding in the wing of majesty that centered around Princess Meresankh. He imagined her hearing the violent beating of his heart as it pounded with love and passion. He was afraid to turn his head toward her, but he saw her gorgeous face in his mind's eye, and in the emptiness that spread out before him. He beheld her radiance despite the drab tones on the horizon, which announced the approach of nightfall.

If only she would bestow upon him a word of thanks like the others, he would deem it above all glory and the world together!

2 3

The crown prince was serious when he said that he would reward Djedef for saving his life. The Fates seemed to have chosen Khafra from among all men to pave the fortunate youth's road to glory. And indeed, but a few days had passed after the incident while hunting when Pharaoh received his heir apparent, among whose close cohorts was Djedef son of Bisharu. This was a more delightful surprise than anything for which the inspector's son had dared hope or dream. Nonetheless, he walked behind Prince Khafra with a heart steadied by surpassing courage, traversing the long corridors with their towering columns and colossal guards, until they appeared before him whose majesty made heads turn away.

Reclining on the throne, the king did not display his now-advanced age except with a few white hairs thrusting out from beneath the double crown of Egypt, and the slight withering of his cheeks. There was also a change in the look of his eyes, shifting away from the sharpness of power and coercion to the contemplation of wisdom and knowledge.

The prince kissed his great father's hand. "Here, my lord," he said, "is the brave officer, Djedef son of Bisharu, whose astounding courage saved my life from the claws of certain death. He has come before you as your sacred will desired."

Pharaoh leaned forward to offer him his hand, and the youth kissed it, kneeling in deep religious respect. "By your valor, O Officer," Khufu said to him, "you have merited my satisfaction."

"My lord, Your Majesty," Djedef said, with a tremulous voice, "as one of the king's soldiers I know of no higher goal than to sacrifice my life for the sake of the throne, and my homeland."

Here Prince Khafra intervened. "I beg my lord the King's permission to appoint this officer chief of my guards."

The young man's eyes widened—he was caught completely unawares. The king answered the prince by asking Djedef, "How old are you, Officer?"

"Twenty years old, Your Majesty," he replied.

Khafra saw the reason for Pharaoh's question. "Long life, wisdom, and knowledge are virtues befitting the priests, O lord," he said. "As for the intrepid warrior, he disdains the limitations of age."

"Whatever you want is yours, Khafra," said the king, smiling. "You are my heir apparent: I cannot deny your wish."

Djedef threw himself down at Pharaoh's feet and kissed his curved staff. At this, Khufu said to him, "I congratulate you for his Pharaonic Highness Prince Khafra's confidence in you, O Commander Djedef son of Bisharu."

Djedef swore an oath of loyalty to the king, and the audience ended. The young man left Pharaoh's palace as one of the commanders of the Egyptian army.

This was a day of unparalleled joy in the house of Bisharu, as Nafa told Djedef, "My prophecy came true. Let me paint you in your commander's uniform."

But Bisharu interrupted him with his coarse voice, now even thicker after the loss of four teeth. "Your prediction didn't produce Djedef," he declared, "rather, it was his father's firmness, in that the gods fated him to be the son of a father among those who are close to Pharaoh."

Zaya never laughed or cried as she did on that ecstatic

day. Her thoughts drifted back to the darkness of the distant past, enfolded in twenty years gone by. She remembered the tiny infant whose birth gave rise to perilous prophecies, stirring a small war in which his true father had fallen victim: Oh, what memories!

When Djedef withdrew unto himself that evening, he fell into a peculiar mood of grief and apprehension, as though in reaction to the transcendent joy that had overfilled the whole day. Yet there were other reasons for it that did not cease to gnaw at his heart, as flame consumes chaff. He stared at the stars in the heavens through his window and sighed, "You alone, O stars," he thought, "know that the heart of Djedef—the happy commander—is more intensely gloomy than the darkness in whose immortal depths you dwell."

2 4

The following day, Djedef took his glorious position as chief of the heir apparent's guards. The prince had improved things by transferring the senior officers of his guard to different formations in the army, replacing them with others. The men received their new head with hospitality, respect, and awe, and he had hardly settled in the commander's chair in his new chamber when Officer Sennefer asked his permission to enter. Djedef granted it and the man came in, his face flushed, giving Djedef a military salute.

"O Chief," said Sennefer, "my heart was not satisfied with just the usual official congratulations, so I sought you out, so that I might tell you personally of my admiration and affection for you."

Djedef smiled fondly at him as he replied gently, "I appreciate these noble feelings fully, but I've done nothing to deserve your thanks."

Moved, Sennefer said, "Perhaps this, my friend, will console me for the loss of your treasured companionship."

"Our comradeship will not end," the young man rejoined, still smiling, "because I intended from the first moment to make you my deputy."

Joyfully, Sennefer declared, "I will not leave your side, O Leader, in good times or bad."

Several days later, Djedef was invited to a meeting with the crown prince—for the first time—as the chief of his guards. And it was the first time that he would be alone with Khafra, observing up close the grimness of his expression and the severity of his features.

As a matter of habit, the prince went straight to his main point immediately. "I am announcing to you now, O Commander," he said with purpose, "that you are summoned, along with the leaders of the army and governors of the provinces, to a meeting hosted by His Majesty the King, for consultation about Mt. Sinai. The order has been given that we will fight the tribes of Sinai. After long hesitation, the will to plunge into the hardships of war has at last been fortified. Egypt will once more see her sons massing—not to build another pyramid—but to put paid to the desert nomads who threaten the safety of the Blessed Valley."

Zealously, Djedef replied, "Permit me, Your Highness, to offer to your lofty dignity my congratulations for the success of your policy."

The iron features smiled. "I am so enormously confident of your valor, O Djedef," Khafra said, "that I'm keeping a pleasant surprise for you, that I will reveal to you after the declaration of war."

Djedef returned from his encounter with the prince in a lighthearted mood, asking himself what this pleasant surprise that Khafra promised him could be. True, the prince had raised him up in the blink of an eye from a minor officer to a mighty commander. So what other good news of glory and happiness could he be hiding? Does his fortune hold in store for him new reasons for pride and joy?

The day of the great meeting arrived. The commanders and governors of Upper and Lower Egypt all came, as Pharaoh's reception hall saw the chiefs of the nation on an equal footing, like the beads of a necklace, to the right of the unshakeable throne, and to its left. The governors sat in one row and the commanders in another, the princes and ministers taking their places behind the throne. The heir apparent sat in the center of the princes, while the priest Hemiunu occupied the same place among the ministers. Sitting at the head of the governors was Prince Ipuwer, while across from him sat Supreme Commander Arbu, chief of the military leadership, whose hair, like the king's, had now turned white.

The chief chamberlain of the palace proclaimed the arrival of His Pharaonic Majesty. Everyone present stood up; the commanders gave a military salute, and the governors and ministers bowed their heads in obeisance. Khufu sat down, granting permission to the others to take their seats. The king wore a band of lion skin over his shoulders, so that all those who had not known it before, saw that Pharaoh had invited them for a council of war.

The meeting was short, but gravely decisive. Pharaoh was strong and vigorous, and his eyes regained their luster of old. He told the great men of his kingdom, in his overpowering voice that filled those who heard it with reverence and awe: "O governors and commanders, I have invited you because of a momentous matter, upon which hangs the safety of our country and the security of our faithful subjects. His Highness Prince Ipuwer, governor of Arsina, has informed me that the tribes of the Sinai continue to attack the outlying villages, and to threaten the caravans of the traders. Experience tells us that the police are not able to subdue them sufficiently to rid the country of their wickedness, for they lack the means to invade the strongholds by which these men are protected. The time has come to destroy these redoubts and to put down the rebels, to drive away their evil from our most loyal people, and to affirm the authority of Pharaoh's government."

Those assembled listened to their lord with a fearsome silence, intensely alert, their faces plainly fascinated, their resolve showing in their pursed lips and glittering eyes. The king turned toward Arbu and asked, "General, is the army ready to carry out its duty?"

The stern commander rose to his feet. "Your Majesty, King of Upper and Lower Egypt, source of power and life," he began, "a hundred thousand soldiers, stationed between the North and the South, are in complete readiness for combat, with countless more troops available, led by battle-hardened chiefs. And double this number could be conscripted in only a short time."

Straightening on his throne, Khufu said, "We, Pharaoh of Upper and Lower Egypt, Khufu son of Khnum, Protector of the Nile and Lord over the Land of Nubia, declare war upon the tribes of Sinai. We order the leveling of their forts, the subjugation of their men, and the capture of their women. And we command you, O governors, to return to your nomes, and that each of you contribute a troop from the guards of his province."

The king pointed to Supreme Commander Arbu, who approached his sovereign, and Khufu said to him, "Note that I do not wish the number of fighting troops to exceed twenty thousand."

Pharaoh rose quickly to his feet. All those present stood as well, calling out his name with great zeal. The fateful meeting came to a close.

Djedef returned on the heels of the crown prince, who was pleased and delighted more than usual. The young man did not doubt then he was rejoicing in the success of his policy, and that he would obtain the objective for which he had so long prepared. Then he remembered what the prince had promised him, and he wavered between perplexity and anticipation, hoping that the prince would honor his pledge.

Yet Khafra did not leave him in this state for long. As he entered his palace, he remarked to Djedef, "I promised you a pleasant surprise—so be informed that I have obtained the king's permission to select you as the commander of the campaign to the Sinai."

25

All of Egypt, from the furthest south to the furthest north, was swept with frenzied activity on a massive scale. Soldiers were assembling everywhere, great ships plowed the waves of the Nile coming from both upstream and down, carrying troops, weapons, and supplies. They were bound for mighty Memphis of the White Walls, where they jammed the capital's barracks and markets, and made the air resound with the clanking of their heavy armaments and the melodies of their fervent anthems. Everyone near and far knew that war was at the gates, and that the children of the Nile would rally to defend their homeland.

Prince Ipuwer returned to his province on business concerning the war. Djedef took the news of his departure mindful of the inevitable worries and misgivings this might cause. He asked himself, "Has the prince won in his personal life what he has garnered in public affairs? Will he go home to his nome happy with the declaration of war and of a pact of love, as well? What had happened between him and the proud and dignified Princess Meresankh? What romantic scenes were witnessed in the thickets of Pharaoh's garden? What secret talk and whispers of love were heard by its birds? Did they watch the arrogant princess humbled before the law that knows no mercy, nor deals gently with haughtiness? Did they hear her moans of passion from that tongue accustomed to command and forbid?"

Djedef's forbearance faltered. Tomorrow he would go to do battle. He would go fearless of death, with a spirit embracing danger and yearning for adventures and thrills. If only he might achieve victory for his homeland and pay with his life for triumph and glory. If only he could perform his duty as a soldier, then take the eternal rest that his tortured heart demanded. What a gorgeous thought to gull the courageous soul, just as he was deceived by his faith in illusory love. Yet he wondered, how could he bid the final farewell to his homeland, without having won a parting look from her? Had his love just been an entertainment, a game? His heart so painfully craved to meet hers, and a glint of her eyes would be dearer to him than the light of sight, the gift of hearing, or the goodness of life. "Do I feel the joys of the world and the pleasures of life except through the radiance of her luminous face?" he asked himself. There was no alternative but to see her and speak to her; this would be difficult for any living being, yet how much easier for one who sought death?

The young commander did not know how he would realize his longed-for desire. The time for getting ready passed very swiftly, until there came that day when it was decided that the army would march on the following morning. The gods chose to grant him ease after his tribulations, and to bring near to him that for which he had so long suffered. Hence, the princess came to pay a surprise visit to her brother, while Khafra had gone to inspect the troops' barracks. The chief of the guards learned of the princess's progress and flew off in haste to await her arrival. Meresankh was not absent for long within the palace when her enchanting face appeared as the chief chamberlain bid her farewell. The youth received her with a forwardness that he had not shown in her presence, except one time only on the banks of the Nile. He gave her a military salute, then escorted her by himself after the chamberlain remained within the palace entrance. He kept two steps behind her, and was able to fill his eyes with the comeliness of her figure, the gracefulness of her form, and the charm of her movements. Inflamed with emotion, he wanted to spread himself on the ground beneath her feet. Then he would feel the fall of her footsteps, the touch of her fingertips, and the rhythm of her breathing in his innermost heart. How amazing! Nature, in her wisdom, hardly lacks a sense of humor. Look at this soldier, how she endows him with victory over the most gargantuan foes. And look at Meresankh, how he bends his neck to this marvelous, delicate creature, who was not made for the rigors of war!

They traversed the long promenade decorated on each side with roses and fragrant flowers, statues, and obelisks, with unhurried steps. The pharaonic boat loomed in the distance, moored at the end of the garden steps. Worry gripped the young man: it seemed impossible to him that she would leave without a word of farewell. He grew anxious to deliver the speech that he wanted to make to her beloved ears. Yet her indifference offered him no opportunity to speak, as he saw the path growing shorter and the ship drawing ever closer. More and more desperate, a moment of recklessness overcame him and loosened the knot around his tongue.

"How happy I am to see you, Your Highness," he said, with a quavering voice, "before our departure tomorrow."

She seemed surprised when he spoke. "You have reached, O Commander, a high position," she said, glaring at him with a look both cruel and bewildered. "So why do I see you gambling with your glory and your future?"

"My glory and my future, Your Highness?" he replied, disdainfully. "Death renders them both meaningless."

"I see that my father has put at the head of his army a commander who is obsessed by the despairs of Death, rather than by victory and triumph," she answered with scorn.

"I am aware of my duty, Your Highness," he said with pride, his handsome face flushing, "and I shall carry it out as befits an Egyptian commander whom the gods have honored by granting him the trust of his sovereign. And I shall sacrifice my life as the price of that trust."

"The man of courage does not forget his past, nor does he violate his traditions, even unto death."

The foolhardy spirit prevailed over him for an instant longer when he said, "This is true, but what is my life if these traditions prevent my tongue from expressing what beats in my heart? I'm leaving tomorrow, and I prayed to the gods that I would see you before going away. My wish was granted—so how could I repudiate the divine favor with cowardly silence?"

"It would be better for you if you learned the virtue of silence."

"After I have said one word."

"What do you want to say?"

His ardor plain on his face, he blurted, "I love you, My Mistress. I loved you the moment I first laid eyes upon you. This is a solemn fact: the courage to express it to Your Highness would not have come to me if it weren't for its transcendent power within me. I beg your pardon, Your Highness."

"This is what you call one word?" she replied, mockingly. "Regardless, what good can your speech do you, when I heard it before one troublesome day on the bank of the Nile?"

She jolted both him and his memory by saying "on the bank of the Nile." So he replied, "I never tire of repeating those words for one minute of my life, O My Mistress, for it is the most vital thing that my tongue can say, the most beautiful thing my ears have heard."

They had reached the marbled steps. Anxiety seized him again, as he said with fervor, "And what shall you say for farewell?"

"I call upon the gods for you, O Commander," she said.

"I pray to Mighty Ptah that you achieve victory for your beloved homeland."

Then she descended the staircase to the boat with deliberateness and dignity.

Djedef continued to look at her with sorrow, watching the craft slowly fade into the distance with a pounding heart. The princess tarried on its deck, rather than entering her compartment, and he fixed his eyes upon her. He kept gazing after her until she vanished at the bend in the river.

Then, with heavy steps, he walked impotently away, headstrong rebellion and a fuming rage massing within him. Yet Djedef possessed a quality that did not let him down in catastrophes, that prevented him from succumbing to emotional reactions that could deflect him from his course or divert him from what he must do. His brother Kheny had taught him how to regard himself critically and to commit himself to the truth and to proper conduct. He excused the princess for her harshness and rigidity, saying to himself that if her sympathies did not incline her toward his suffering, that only meant that she did not share his feelings—nor was she obliged to love him. His bitter disappointment need mean nothing to her. Rather, he should accept this with kindness and mercy. Did he not say to her what cannot be said to a princess of Pharaoh's household? And what did she do about it? Nothing—but to hear him out and forgive him beautifully. If she wished, she could destroy him with disgrace, and reduce him to the lowest of the low! His thoughts helped to quell his heart, but they did not assuage his frustration in the least—and he was enveloped in a sad, painful silence.

———

He spent that evening in Bisharu's house, saying goodbye to his family. He tried his best to display the joy and the gaiety that they obliged him to feel. They all gathered around the dinner table: Bisharu, Zaya, Kheny, Nafa and his wife, Mana, and in the center was the youthful commander. They ate tantalizing food washed down with beer, while Bisharu kept talking throughout without stopping, utterly oblivious to the morsels that flew from his toothless mouth. He told them war stories, especially of those wars whose adversities he had faced as a young man, as though to reassure Zaya, whose paleness revealed the fears that surged within her breast.

"The burdens of war mostly fall to the ordinary soldiers," he asserted. "The commanders occupy a safer position, planning and thinking things out."

Djedef understood his purpose. "I believe you, father," he said. "But do you mean that you proved your outstanding courage in the war in Nubia as a minor officer or as a great commander?"

The old man's body stiffened with pride. "At that time I was a low-ranking officer in the spear-throwers' brigade. My record in the war was one of the merits that lay behind my appointment as general inspector of Pharaoh's pyramid."

Bisharu's prattle continued without pause. Djedef would listen to him sometimes, only to drift away distractedly at others. Perhaps the pain overcame him then, and a grief-stricken look would flash in his eyes. Zaya seemed instinctively aware of his sadness, for she was silent and heavy hearted. She did not touch her food, sating herself merely with a flagon of beer at the banquet.

Nafa wanted this night to end happily—so he invited his wife Mana to play the lyre-harp and to sing a charming song, "I Was Triumphant in Love and War." Mana's voice was soft and melodious, and she played with great skill, as she filled the room with the enchanting tune.

Meanwhile, a scorching fire flared in Djedef's heart, whose flames reached none of those present but he himself. Nafa studied him in ignorance and naiveté, drawing close to

Djedef to whisper in his ear, "I bring good news, O Commander. Yesterday you were triumphant in love, and tomorrow you shall be triumphant in war."

"What do you mean by that?" Djedef asked, confused.

The painter grinned slyly. "Do you think that I have forgotten the picture of the beautiful peasant girl? Ah—how lovely are the peasant girls of the Nile! They all dream of lying in the arms of a handsome officer in the green grass on the banks of the river. What would you say if this officer was none other than the seductive Djedef?"

"Quiet, O Nafa," he said indignantly. "You know nothing!"

What Nafa said disturbed him just as Mana's singing had; he felt the desire to flee. He would have acted on his wish if he had not remembered his mother. He glanced at her sideways to find her staring fixedly at him. He feared that she would read the page of his heart with her all-consuming eyes, and that she would be wounded with a great sorrow. So he drew close to her and smiled, deceiving her with merriment and joy.

2 6

Commander Djedef sat in his tent in the military camp outside the walls of Memphis, staring at a map of the Sinai Peninsula, its great wall, and the desert roads that lead to it. The horses neighed and the chariots rattled as the soldiers came and went, all enveloped in the calm azure light of early morning.

Officer Sennefer came into Djedef's tent, saluting him with respect. "A messenger from His Pharaonic Highness Prince Khafra has come," he said, "seeking leave to enter upon you."

"Bid him do so," said Djedef, his interest aroused.

Sennefer disappeared for a moment, then returned with the messenger before again exiting the tent. The messenger wore a priest's ample robe that covered his body from his shoulders to his ankles. On his head was a black cowl, while his thick beard flowed down to the hollow of his chest. Djedef was amazed at the sight of him, because he had expected to encounter a familiar face, one of those that he regularly saw in the crown prince's palace. And then he heard a voice that, despite its faintness, he imagined he was not hearing for the first time.

"I have come, Your Excellency, about a serious matter," said the messenger. "Therefore, I hope that you will order the curtain to be drawn over the doorway, and that you will forbid anyone from entering without your permission."

Djedef stared at the priest with a searching look, pervaded by hesitation. But then he shrugged his massive shoulders dismissively, as though taking the matter lightly. He called out to Sennefer, ordering him to draw shut the flap over the tent's entrance, adding that no person should be permitted to approach it. Sennefer carried out Djedef's commands, and when he departed, Djedef looked at the messenger.

"Give me what you have," he demanded.

When the messenger was sure that they were alone in the tent, he lifted the black cowl from his head. Luxuriant black hair cascaded from under it, the locks falling over his shoulders in a flurry, painting a halo around a marvelous head. Then the messenger's hand reached toward his beard and pulled it off with a refined twist, as he opened his eyes that had been deliberately narrowed. A radiant face appeared, beaming a light through the air of the tent, along with the first rays that the sun sent forth over the desert's vastness outside.

Djedef's heart flew about in his breast, as he exclaimed with a tremulous voice, "My Mistress, Meresankh!"

He rushed toward her like a panicked bird, and knelt at her feet, kissing the fringes of her loose-fitting robe. The princess fixed her gaze in front of her with a timid, bashful expression, while her lissome body trembled. All the while, she felt the young man's hot breath flowing through the fabric of her trousers, blowing upon her perfumed thighs. Then she stroked his head with her fingertips and whispered softly, "Arise," and the young man stood up, his eyes flashing with a joyful, delighted light.

"Is this real, My Mistress? Is it true what I hear? And what I see?" he stammered.

She gazed upon him with a look of surrender as though saying to him, "You have overcome me totally, so I have come to you."

"The gods of joy are singing all at once within me at this

moment. Their songs have accompanied me through these months of torment and their sleepless nights. Their melodies have cleansed my heart of the bitterness of distress and shadows of despair. O Lord! Who would say that I'm the one whom yesterday life had scorned?"

The emotion showed on her face as she said in a shaking voice, like the cooing of a dove, "Did life truly treat you with scorn?"

As his eyes devoured the lips from which her speech had issued, he replied, "Yes, it treated me harshly, and I actually wished for death. The soul who craves death is that which has lost hope. I've never been a coward, My Mistress, so I remained loyal to my duty. Yet the sense of futile triviality tortured me." Then he added, "This and the melancholy weighed heavily upon me, and my eyes were veiled with gloom."

She sighed and rejoined, "I was fighting my pride, struggling with myself, for it tormented me always."

"How cruel you were to me!"

"I was even crueler to myself," she said. "I remember that day on the bank of the Nile. That day a strange unease kept filling my heart. Later I learned that my heart was fated to awake through your voice from its deep slumber. This fact, I discovered, left me split between the thrill of adventure and the fear of the unknown. Then I remembered your nobility and your self-confidence, so I rebelled. And whenever I cast my eyes upon you, I was harsh with myself, and with you, as well."

Then he sighed, and said with yearning, "How I suffered for my vain delusions! Do you remember our second meeting, in His Majesty's palace? You scolded me violently and rebuked me severely. Just yesterday you wouldn't hear out my grievance, and left me without a word of goodbye. Do you know how much agony and pain I have endured? Alas! If only I had known what was to come! My most desolate times would have been my happiest. I pleaded to the gods over my torment. How they must have laughed at my ignorance!"

"And the gods witnessed my arrogance and were amused by my contempt," she said, smiling. "Have you ever seen such a farce as ours before?"

"And when the farce is over, it is time to mourn. All I can think of is the precious time that has been lost to us!" he said.

Groaning regretfully, she said, "The blame is on my head."

He regarded her tenderly. "I would sacrifice myself to protect you from all evil," he said.

Smiling sweetly, she replied, "I think that time is being cruel to us today."

He moaned sorrowfully and peered at her with downcast eyes. So she said as the spirit of hope spread through her being, "There is a long future, lit with hope, lying before us. Wish for life as you once wished for death."

"Death shall never hold sway over my heart," he said, with happiness and joy.

"Don't say this," she said, putting a finger over his mouth.

But then he said, with an insane passion, "What can Death do to a heart that love has made immortal?"

"I shall stay in the palace—I shall not leave it," she vowed, "until I hear the horn sound the tidings of your triumphant return!"

"Let us pray to the gods to shorten our separation!"

"Yes, I'll pray to Ptah, but in the palace, not here," she said, "because we do not have enough time."

As she replaced the cowl on her head, it pained him to see her pitch-black hair disappear once again beneath it.

"I hate to be parted from such a dear limb of my own body," he said.

She looked at him, her eyes glinting with the light of love and expectation. Yet she imagined that his face was growing dark as his breast was pounding, and that his brow was shadowed by storm clouds. Disquiet conquered her as she asked him, "Of what are you thinking?"

"Prince Ipuwer," he answered, tersely.

Laughing, she replied, "Hasn't what the gossips were saying about him some time ago yet reached you? How strange. . . . Nothing is hidden in Egypt, even the secrets of Pharaoh's palace. But you've learned only one thing, while you don't know others. The prince is a sublime person, of virtuous character. He spoke with me one day while we were alone, on the subject that had been announced. I apologized and said to him that I'd be comfortable to remain his friend. No doubt he felt disappointed, but then he smiled his magnanimous smile and told me, 'I love truth and freedom—and I would hate to so demean such a noble soul as yours.'"

Djedef said with exhilaration, "What a magnificent man!"

"Yes, he is decent, indeed."

"Is there not one thing on our horizon that might call for pessimism?" Djedef stuttered. "I mean . . . I do fear Pharaoh!"

She lowered her eyes shyly. "My father would not be the first pharaoh to make one of his subjects a member of his own family."

Her answer delighted him and her shyness intoxicated him. He leaned toward her in painful passion, stretching his hand toward hers—when it was about to reattach the beard to her face—in fear that the gorgeous, luminous visage would vanish. She surrendered her hand to his, and her acquiescence was a bewitching act of sweetness. The young man knelt down again before her, kissing her hand with mad enchantment, as she said to him, "May all the gods be with you!"

Then, putting the false beard back on her chin, and pulling down on the cowl until its edge touched her eyebrows, she returned to her former guise as the crown prince's messenger. Before turning her back to him, she reached within her breast and withdrew the little beloved portrait that nature had made the spark for this beautiful infatuation, and gave it to him wordlessly. He took it with mad love and passion, kissing it with his mouth before burying it in his own breast in its original, familiar place. Then she flashed him a smile of goodbye, before—to make him laugh—giving him a military salute and marching, in soldierly fashion, outside.

The youth that she left reeling with delirium, his face beaming with the light of hope, was not the one she saw at her arrival—dejected, distracted, and confused. His love was aroused once more and revived after it had become lifeless. In that spectacular moment, fantasies of his heart's past visited his imagination—Nafa's lovely gallery; the lush green banks of the Nile; the band of pretty peasant girls. Then he remembered his sadness and despair, and wrapped himself once more in the pelt of patience before recalling the glowing promise that he perceived amidst the flood of despondent sorrow. The reality of life and love seemed to him like a river bearing water to a burgeoning garden, with flowers blooming and birds warbling from the sweetness that it brings. But should its springs dry up, the garden trellises would be bare, its beauty would wither—and it would be nothing more than an abandoned patch of desert.

Sennefer's return snapped him from his reverie. The officer informed him that everything was now ready, so Djedef ordered him to have the horns sound the signal for departure. Immediately a great movement spread throughout the encampment as the music was played and the first units of the army began to march. Djedef mounted the commander's chariot, which was driven by Sennefer. Then the most senior officers mounted their vehicles, and the group of them proceeded to the heart of the troop of chariots. As the horns sounded again, Djedef's chariot moved to the head of the troop, flanked by two wings of mighty officers.

Following them was a formation composed of parallel ranks of three thousand war chariots bristling with weapons. Marching behind them were the brigades of infantrymen, each one bearing its own standard. At their head was the brigade of archers, then the spear-throwers, trailed by the swordsmen. Following the army were huge wagons bearing weapons, provisions, and medical supplies, guarded by a squadron of horsemen.

This army traversed the desert wastes, its destination the mighty wall that the tribes had taken as their secure fortification.

The forenoon sun had risen over them, and the blaze of midday heat had scorched them, when the breeze of sunset struck them as they stalked the earth like giants. The ground almost seemed to complain from bearing their immense weight, while they themselves complained of nothing.

27

A scouting chariot was seen rapidly covering the ground in their direction, and they watched it with great interest. Its commander approached Djedef and informed him that their eyes had detected a band of Bedouin scattered around Tell al-Duma. The reconnaissance officer proposed that a troop of soldiers go out to fight them. Intrigued, Djedef spread out a map of the desert in front of him, searching for Tell al-Duma.

"Tell al-Duma lies to the south of our path," he said. "These Bedouin are known to travel in small parties that pillage and then flee—and it would never enter their minds that they would be attacked by a sizeable army like ours. We have no reason to fear an attempt to outflank us."

One of the officers spoke up. "I think, Your Excellency," he said, "that it would not be wise to leave them as they are."

"No doubt we will stumble upon quite a few groups like this one," the youthful commander countered. "If we sent out a unit of soldiers against each of them, we would disperse our forces, so let's keep our eyes fixed on the primary objective. And that is to pierce the wall around their stronghold in the midst of their territory, and to arrest their leader, Khanu."

Yet Djedef wisely chose to strengthen the force protecting their supplies. Meanwhile, the army advanced on its route, seeing no trace of any tribesmen along the way. News came to them that all those who roamed the desert, when they heard of the approach of the army marching in the peninsula's direction, had turned tail and fled. And so the Egyptians proceeded down the safe, empty road until they reached Arsina.

There they stopped for rest and provisions. Prince Ipuwer came to visit them, and was given a reception befitting his rank. The prince inspected the units of the army, then lingered with the commander and his senior officers, discussing with them the affairs of the campaign. He suggested that they leave a detachment between them and Arsina to communicate their news, and to promptly send them anything they might need. Then he addressed them, "You should know that all the forces in Arsina are buckled up to fight," said Ipuwer, "and that sizeable reinforcements from Serapeum, Dhaqa'a, and Mendes are on their way to Arsina, as well."

"We beseech the gods, O Your Highness," answered Djedef, "that we do not require new troops, respecting the wish of His Majesty, who is anxious to preserve the lives of the believers."

That night the army slept deeply and quietly. Then it awoke to the blast of the horns when the cock began to crow.

Pharaoh's army resumed its march, moving east from Arsina with an awful clamor. They kept stopping for rest, then resuming their journey, until there loomed in the distance the huge wall that began in the south at the Gulf of Hieropolis, then bent eastward, tracing the shape of a great bow. The expedition swung toward the north, then turned slightly to the east before encamping in a spot where assailants' arrows could not reach them.

From their camp, they could observe the firmness of the wall's construction. They could also see the guards perched upon it, bows in hand, ready to defend it against any attacking army.

Djedef and the officers agreed that, in this case, there was no purpose in waiting to launch their assault, as there would be if they intended to take a city by starving its populace. They reached a consensus that it was best to begin with light provocative skirmishes to test their enemy's strength.

Clearly it was dangerous to use their chariots in the first battle for fear of losing their brightly bedecked horses. Therefore, they put hundreds of armored bowmen at the lead, arrayed in a half circle, each one separated by tens of arm's lengths from his nearest fellow. They approached until they reached a point where the enemy thought that it was practical to launch their arrows at them, and they judged it effective to respond in kind. Thus began the first battle between the two sides, the arrows flying in dense droves, like clouds of locusts, most of them vanishing into the great void between them.

Djedef watched the battle with absolute concentration, admiring the Egyptians' skill in archery that had long won them a reputation without peer. Then he spied the gate on the wall.

"What a massive portal that is," he said to Sennefer, "as though it were the entrance to the Temple of Ptah!"

"Just wide enough for our chariots when we punch through it later," the zealous officer replied.

The skirmish was not in vain. Djedef noticed that the tribesmen had not built towers on the fortress's walls from which to shoot arrows down on their attackers. As a result, their bowmen could not respond without exposing themselves to danger. Hence, it seemed profitable to attack with great armored shields, known as "the domes." Shaped like the prayer niches in the walls of temples, and big enough to cover a soldier from his head to his feet, they each had a small aperture near the top, through which the soldiers fired their arrows. Thanks to their thick plating, the only way these shields could be penetrated was through these same openings.

Djedef ordered several hundred of the men carrying these shields to advance on the wall's defenders. The soldiers were all to line up behind their armor in the form of a wide half circle. They all then moved up toward the wall, indifferent to the hail of arrows falling down upon them. Next, they set their shields on the ground and fired their own arrows, as a fierce and bloody battle began between them and their enemy, the messengers of death flying to and from both sides. The tribesmen succumbed in great numbers, but they nonetheless displayed a strange steadfastness and a rare sort of valor. Each time a group of them fell, another took its place. And despite the Egyptians' protection behind their peculiar armor, many were struck by missiles piercing the tiny apertures, and were killed or wounded as a result.

The vicious combat continued until the western horizon was stained with the blood red glow of evening. Then commands went out for the Egyptians to fall back, when exhaustion had sapped them of all that it could.

28

Memphis awaited news of the Sinai campaign with a confident calm, due to the overwhelming trust she had in the great nation's army, and her overweening contempt for the marauding Bedouin tribes. Yet great hearts still feared for the fate of those fighting on Egypt's behalf.

Among them was the mighty monarch of the Nile, who, in his old age, had turned toward wisdom as he continued to compose, from the inkwell of his soul, his immortal message to his beloved people. Another was Zaya, consumed by pain, tormented by dread, and haunted by insomnia. And there was another heart, which had not before known the meaning of agony or the bitter taste of terror. This belonged to Princess Meresankh, whom the gods had endowed with the most splendid beauty on earth, and with the most pleasing opulence and comfort, rendering the most magnificent of all human hearts subservient to her affection. The gods went so far as to hold her harmless from the powers of nature: the cold of winter did not sting her, the heat of summer did not sear her; the wind from the South did not fall upon her, nor did the rain from the North. All the while she had continued to sport and play until her heart was touched by love, as the newborn infant's fingertips are first touched by flame. Burned by the fire, she opened her breast to its torture, and its humiliation.

Her condition was noted by her handmaidens, and by her servant Nay in particular. One day Nay said to her, as she observed her with a fearful, worried eye, "Did you sigh, My Mistress? What then, would one do, if they were not one to whom the gods and the pharaohs pay heed? Are you kneeling down to beg and plead? But to whom, then, can we do the same? You're lowering your eyes, My Mistress? But for whom was your haughtiness made?"

Yet the princess's dream held no room for her servant's banter. During those long, empty, difficult days, all she thought of was her own plight. If she had been able, she would have wanted to keep to what she said to her sweetheart—that she would not leave the palace until she heard the horns blowing the call of his triumphant return. Yet she found herself yearning to visit the palace of her brother, the heir apparent, to pay a heartfelt tribute to the place where her love used to meet her whenever she came.

When the crown prince received her, he did not conceal feelings that she had not known of before. These were his discontent over the king's policies, to the point that he told her angrily, "Our father is becoming senile very quickly."

She looked at him with disbelief. "True," Khafra continued, "he has preserved his physical health and the sharpness of his mind. Yet his heart is getting old and feeble. Don't you see that he's turning his back on state policy, distracted—in both his heart and his mind—by meditation and compassion? He spends his precious time writing! Where is this found among the duties of the powerful ruler?"

"Compassion, like power, is among the virtues of the perfect sovereign," she replied with irritation.

"My father did not teach me this saying, Meresankh," he answered sarcastically. "Instead, he taught me immortal examples of the monuments of creative power, the most majestic of works. He utilized the nation of believers to build his pyramid, to move mountains and to tame the recalcitrant rocks. He roared like the marauding lion, and hearts dropped down submissively in horror and fright, and souls approached him, out of obedience—or from hate. He would kill whomever he pleased. That was my father, whom I miss, and whom I do not find. I see nothing but that old man who passes all but a few nights in his burial chamber, pondering and dictating. That old man who avoids war, and who feels for his soldiers as though they were made for something other than fighting."

"Do not speak of Pharaoh this way, O Prince," said Meresankh. "Our father served our homeland in the days when he was strong. And he will go on serving it doubly so—with his wisdom."

Yet not all her visits to the prince's palace were spent in conversations like this one. For, when twenty days had passed since the Egyptian army's departure, she found the heir apparent pleased and happy. As she looked at him, she saw the tough features soften briefly with a smile, and her heart fluttered, her thoughts flying away to her distant sweetheart.

"What's behind this, O Your Highness?" she asked her brother.

"The wonderful news has reached me that our army has won some outstanding victories," he said. "Soon they will take the enemy's fortress."

She cried out to him, "Do you have more of this happy news to tell me?"

"The messenger says that our soldiers advanced behind their shields until they came to within an arm's length of the wall—on which it was impossible for the tribesmen to appear without being hit. And so our arrows brought many of them down."

This was the happiest news she had heard from her brother in her life. She left the prince's palace headed for the Temple of Ptah, and prayed to the mighty lord that the army would be victorious and her sweetheart safe. She remained deeply immersed in prayer for a long time, in the way that only lovers know. But as she returned to Pharaoh's palace, unease crept into her heart—whose patience diminished the closer she came to its goal.

29

The Egyptian troops had gotten so close to the fortress's wall that they could touch it with the tips of their spears. Faced by marksmen all around, each time a man appeared on it, they would sight him with their bows—and fell him. There was no means left for the enemy but to throw rocks down upon them, or to hunt with their arrows anyone who tried to scale the wall. Things remained in this state for a time, each side lying in wait for his adversary. Then at dawn on the twenty-fifth day of siege, Djedef issued his order to the archers to make a general attack. They broke into two groups: one to watch the wall, and the other to advance bearing wooden ladders, protected by their great shields, and armed with bows and arrows. They leaned their ladders against the wall and climbed up, holding their shields before them like standards. Then they secured their shields on top of the wall, making it look like the rampart of an Egyptian citadel armored with "domes." Once on the wall they were met with thousands of arrows, shot at them from every direction, and more than a few men perished. They answered their enemy's fire, continuously filling the air with the terrifying whoosh of their lethal shafts, as loud cries pierced the clouds in the sky, the cheers of hitting a target mixing with the moans of pain and the screams of fear. During the desperate struggle, a group of foot soldiers attacked the great gate with battering rams made from the trunks of date palms. They rattled it immensely, creating an appalling din.

Djedef stood astride his war chariot, surveying the battle apprehensively, his heart braced for combat. His head turned from side to side as he shifted his gaze from the soldiers scaling the wall and those rushing to do so, then to the men assaulting the towering doorway whose four corners had begun to loosen, and whose frame to throb.

After some time, he saw the archers leaping down inside the wall. Then he saw the infantrymen, their spears at the ready, climbing the ladders, brandishing their shields. He then knew that the enemy had started to abandon an area behind the wall, and was retreating within the peninsula.

Hours of grueling combat and anxious suspense went by. The squadron of chariots—the young commander at its lead—was waiting tensely, when suddenly the gate flew open after the Egyptian troops inside the wall raised its bolt. The horses were given free rein as the vehicles charged through it, with a rumble like the sound of a falling mountain, kicking up a gale of dust and sand behind them. One by one they flew past the portal, this going to the right, that to the left, forming two broad wings that joined behind the commander's chariot.

They smote the enemy as a massive fist mashes a fragile bird, while the bowmen seized all the fortified positions and the overlooking hills. Meanwhile, the spearmen moved forward behind them to protect the chariots, and to fight whoever doubled back to encircle them.

The decisive engagement ended in just a few hours. The tribesmen's villages spent that night at the mercy of the occupying army. The ground was strewn with the bodies of those killed or wounded, as the soldiers roamed here and there without any order. The Egyptians devoted themselves to searching among the corpses for their brothers in battle who had fallen on the field of honor. They kept carrying them to the encampment outside the wall, while others gathered the remains of the enemy dead in order to count them. Yet others bound the prisoners with ropes as they stripped them of their weapons, lining them up, row upon row. Then the little hamlets were emptied of their women and children and bunched into different groups, where they screamed and wailed beside their captured menfolk, guards surrounding them on every side. As the troops returned, each went to where the standard of his own unit was raised. The brigades then stood in formation, all headed by officers that had made it through the scourge of battle alive.

The commander came, followed by the leaders of the brigades, and reviewed the victorious army that saluted him with a prodigious fervor. He greeted his gallant officers, congratulating them for their success and their survival, as he paid tribute to those who had given themselves as martyrs. Then he walked with his war chiefs to the spot where the cadavers of the fallen foe were thrown. Some of their bodies were stretched out next to each other; their blood flowed from them in rivers. Djedef found a detachment watching over them, and asked the officer in command, "How many killed and wounded?"

"Three thousand enemy killed, and five thousand wounded," the man replied.

"And our losses were how many?"

"One thousand of our own killed, and three thousand wounded."

The youth's face darkened. "Have the Bedouin tribes cost us so dear?" he wondered aloud.

Next, the commander went to see the place where the prisoners were held. They were gathered under guard, the long ropes splitting them into groups, their arms tied behind their backs, their heads bent down until their beards touched their breasts. Djedef glanced at them, then said to those around him, "They shall work the mines of Qift that complain of being short of labor, where they'll be glad indeed to get these strong men."

He and his consort then moved on to a raucous area, from which there was no escape, where the noncombatant captives were kept. The children bawled and cried, as the parents slapped their faces and shrieked at them. The women beat their own faces, lamenting their menfolk who were killed or wounded, or taken prisoner, or gone fugitive. While Djedef did not know their language, he gazed at them from his chariot with a look not lacking in sympathy. His sight fell upon a band of them who seemed more affluent than the rest.

"Who are these women?" he asked the officer supervising their guards.

"They're the harem of the tribesmen's leader," answered the officer.

The commander considered them with a smile. They regarded him with cold eyes, which no doubt concealed behind them a blazing fire, wishing that they could overpower this conquering commander who had taken them and their master captive—and who had turned them from privileged persons into the lowest of the low in a single blow.

One of them broke free from the others and wanted to approach the commander. Between her and her goal was a soldier, who signaled to her threateningly—but she called out to Djedef in clear Egyptian, "O Commander, let me come close to you, and may the Lord Ra bless you!"

Djedef was dumbfounded, as they all were, at what issued from her tongue—she spoke Egyptian with a native accent. The commander ordered the soldier to let her approach him. She did so with slow, deliberate steps until she neared the youth, then bowed before him in deference and respect. She was a woman of fifty, of dignified appearance, her face showing the traces of an ancient beauty that time and misery had destroyed. Her features bore an uncanny resemblance to the daughters of the Nile.

"I see that you know our language, madam," Djedef addressed her.

The woman was moved so intensely that her eyes drowned in tears. "How could I not know it, since I was raised to know no other?" she said. "I am Egyptian, my lord."

The young man's astonishment increased and he felt a powerful sympathy for her. "Are you truly an Egyptian, my lady?"

She answered with sadness and certainty, "Yes, sir—an Egyptian, daughter of Egyptians."

"And what brought you here?"

"What brought me here was my wretched luck, that I was kidnapped in my youth by these uncouth, uncivilized men, who obtained their just portion at your courageous hands. The vilest torment was inflicted upon me until their leader rescued me from their evil—only to afflict me with his own. He added me to his harem, where I suffered the debasement of being a prisoner—which I endured for twenty years."

This roused Djedef's emotions even further. "Today, your captivity ends, my lady, who are bound to me by race and nation," he told the despairing woman. "So be gladdened."

The woman to whom time had been so cruel for twenty long years sighed. She wanted to kneel at the commander's feet, but he grasped her hand empathetically. "Be at ease, my lady. From what town do you come?"

"From On, my lord—the residence of Our Lord Ra."

"Don't be sad that the Lord subjected you to twenty years of evil, out of wisdom known only to Him," he said. "Yet He did not forget you. I will recount your story to My Lord the King and petition him to set you free, so that you may return to your native district, happy and content."

Anxiously the woman pleaded, "I beg you, sir, please send me to my hometown at once. The gods may grant that I will find my family."

But the youth shook his head. "Not before I raise your case with Pharaoh—for you, and this applies to all the prisoners—are the king's property, and we must invariably render those things entrusted to our care to their rightful owner. Yet be reassured, and do not fear anything, for Pharaoh, Lord of the Egyptians, will neither keep them as captives nor humiliate them." He wanted to restore confidence to this tortured soul, hence he sent her to his camp, honored with great esteem.

When evening came that day the army had finished burying its dead and dressing the wounds of the injured. The men repaired to their tents to take their ration of rest after the fatigue of the exhausting day. Djedef sat in front of the entrance to his own tent, warming himself by the fire and contemplating his surroundings with dreamy eyes. On the earth, the greatest thing moving him was the sight of the Egyptian standards mounted over the wall of the fortress; in the sky, it was those stars that were like eyes sparkling miraculously for eternity by the power of the Creator and the splendor of creation. Lovely visions hovered in the heaven of his imagination, like these stars—standing in his heart for his happy memories of Memphis and the dreams that they conjured. In his rapture, he did not forget that solemn moment soon approaching when he would stand before Pharaoh and ask for the heart of the dearest creature to himself in Egypt. What a grave moment that would be! Yet, how beautiful life would be if he were propelled from triumph to triumph, transported from happiness to happiness. May it go that way always! If only the Fates would have mercy on man. But the obvious reality is that happiness is scarce in this world. And could he ever forget the image of that woman of rare pride, whom the Bedouin had kidnapped amidst her own happiness, stolen her youth, and made her endure oppression for all of twenty years? How outrageous!

Yes, Djedef was unable, amidst his own happiness and triumph, to forget that woman's wretchedness.

3 o

As the sun rose over Memphis of the White Walls, the city looked as though she was hosting one of the great fetes dedicated to the Lord Ptah. The flags waved over the roofs of the houses and mansions. The roads and squares surged with the masses of people as if they were the billows of the Nile during the yearly flood. The air resounded with anthems of greeting for Pharaoh, his triumphant army, and its heroic soldiers.

The branches of palm and olive trees flapped about like the wings of a genial bird, caressing heads crowned with victory as it warbled with joy. And through this elated melee, the processions of princes, ministers, and priests pressed their way to the city's northern gate, to receive the victorious forces and their valiant commander.

At the appointed hour, the breeze brought them the tunes of the conquering army, as its forward units, their banners flapping, appeared on the horizon. The cheers went up as the people clapped and waved the branches with their hands. The crowd overflowed with a tide of fervid enthusiasm that made it seem like a roiling sea.

The army advanced in its customary order, led by the bands of prisoners, their arms bound and chins lowered. These were followed by the great wagons carrying the captive women and children, and the spoils of conquest. Then came the squadron of chariots headed by the young commander, surrounded by the important men of the realm who had come to receive him. Next were the lines of mighty war chariots in their exacting array, and, immediately after them, the archers, spearmen, and bearers of light weapons. All of them proceeded to the strains of their own music, leaving gaps in their ranks for those who had fallen, in salute to their memory and their noble martyrdom for the sake of their homeland and sovereign.

Djedef was blissful and proud, gazing into the impassioned crowd with gleaming eyes, returning the warm salutations with sweeps of his awesome sword. His eyes plumbed the masses for the beloved faces of those whom he never doubted would cry out his name when they saw him. He even imagined for a moment that he heard the voice of his mother, Zaya, and the bellow of his vain and boastful father, Bisharu. His heart pounded violently as he wondered if those two dark eyes that inspired him with love, as the emerging sun inspires the hearts of the Egyptians to worship the divine presence, now looked upon him. Does she see him in his hour of glory? Does she hear his name cheered by the thronging thousands? Does she recognize his face, pale from separation and longing?

The army continued on its way to the Great House of Pharaoh. The king and queen stepped out onto the balcony overlooking the huge square known as the Place of the People. Below them paraded the prisoners of war, the wagons full of booty, the civilian captives, and the divisions of the army. Then, as Djedef approached the royal balcony, he pulled out his sword, stretching his arm out in salute, and turned to face Khufu and his wife. Behind them stood the princesses Henutsen, Neferhetepheres, Hetepheres—and Meresankh. His eyes were drawn to those bewitching orbs that held a power over him unlike anything else in creation. Their eyes exchanged a burning message of ardent desire and consuming passion, and if, on its path between them, it had brushed against the hem of one of the banners, it would have burst into an engulfing flame.

Commander Djedef was called to appear before Pharaoh, and—steady and confident—he obeyed. Once again, as he came into His Majesty's presence, the king leaned toward him, putting forward his staff. Djedef prostrated himself to kiss it, then laid the bolt to the gate of the forbidding wall that his victorious army had sundered at the foot of the throne.

"My Lord, His Majesty Pharaoh of Upper and Lower Egypt, Sovereign of the Eastern and Western Deserts, and Master of the Land of Nubia," he declaimed, "Sire! The gods have lent their strength to a mighty task and a striking conquest. For a group that until yesterday were rebellious bullies has now been brought forcibly into your obedience. Beneath the sheltering wings of your divinity, the humbled now huddle in misery, swearing, in their demeaning captivity, their pledge of fealty to your indomitable throne."

The king, his head crowned with white hair, said to him, "Pharaoh congratulates you, O triumphant Commander, for your integrity and your valor. He wishes that the gods may lengthen your life, so that the homeland may continue to benefit from your gifts."

Khufu bent forward, offering his hand to the youthful commander, who kissed it in profound respect.

"How many of my soldiers sacrificed themselves for the sake of their homeland and Pharaoh?" asked the king.

"One thousand heroes were martyred," answered Djedef, his voice subdued.

"And the number of wounded?"

"Three thousand, my lord."

Pharaoh paused for a moment. "Great life requires great sacrifice," he said. "May the Lord be praised, Who creates life out of death."

He looked at Djedef for a long while before saying, "You have rendered me two magnificent services. In the first, you saved the life of my heir apparent. And in the second, you rescued the well-being of my people. So what, then, is your request?"

"My God!" Djedef thought. "The horrendous hour has come that my soul has always desired, that I have always pictured in my happiest dreams." Yet, ever an intrepid lad, he did not lose his nerve even in the most daunting situations.

"My lord," he said, "what I did in those two instances was the duty of any soldier, so I do not ask that you grant them any reward. Yet I do have a wish, that I present as one hoping for the compassion of his king."

"What is your wish?"

"The divinities, sire, in their ineffable wisdom, have summoned my ordinary human heart to the heavens of my sire the king, where it clings to the feet of Princess Meresankh!"

Pharaoh peered at him strangely. "But what have the gods wrought in the heart of the Princess?" he asked.

Mortified, Djedef took refuge in a heavy silence.

The king smiled.

"They say that a servant never enters the sanctuary of the Lord unless he is sure to bring him contentment," he said. "We shall see whether or not this is true!"

Khufu was pleased, and as though for a bit of entertainment, he sent for Princess Meresankh. At her father's summons, the princess came gliding in the glory of her loveliness. When she saw the one she loved standing before him, her being throbbed with shyness and confusion, as she balked like a gazelle that had chanced upon a man.

Pharaoh gazed at her with sympathy, saying to her tenderly, but sarcastically, as well, "O Princess! This commander boasts that he has conquered two fortresses: the wall of Sinai—and your heart!"

"My lord!" Djedef called out, in shocked entreaty.

But he was unable to say more and so kept quiet, defeated and dismayed. Khufu looked at the commander, whose bravery had betrayed him. He looked at the princess, whose arrogance had deserted her, weakened by bewilderment and timidity. His heart went out to her, as he called her to his side. Then he called Djedef to him, as well, and the youth drew near in dreadful fear.

The king laid the hand of the princess into Djedef's hand with slow deliberation, and said in his most awesome voice, which made hearts shiver, "I bless you both in the name of the gods."

In the twelve hours immediately following his fortuitous audience with Pharaoh, Djedef experienced great and peculiar events that shook souls to their core and shattered minds completely. In what had fleetingly seemed the promise of a serene, carefree life, they came like the turbulence of a cataract in the stately, majestic course of the Nile.

What did Djedef do during this brief interlude, so full of strange occurrences?

Upon leaving the Pharaonic presence, he requested a meeting with the vizier Hemiunu, whom he briefed on the subject of the unlucky Egyptian lady that he held prisoner, and who was never out of his thoughts. The kindly vizier cleared the way, discharging her to the commander's care.

"I congratulate you, my lady," said Djedef, "for the return of your freedom after being so long in captivity. As the hour is late, you shall stay as my guest until tomorrow, then you will set your face in the direction of On, in the protection of the gods."

She seized his hand and kissed it with great thankfulness, then raised up her face, and her tears were flowing over her cheeks and her neck. He accompanied the woman as they walked to his chariot, where he saw Sennefer awaiting him close by. Saluting Djedef, the officer told him, "His Pharaonic Highness Prince Khafra has charged me to inform the commander of his wish to speak with him right away."

Djedef asked him, "Where is His Highness now?"

"In his palace."

Djedef took Sennefer and the woman together in his chariot to the crown prince's palace. When they arrived, he asked the lady to wait for him where she was. Then he went into the palace with Sennefer behind him. He asked to see the prince, and was invited into his chamber. He found the young man not as he usually was, but intensely disturbed, trying to gain control of himself. This time, Khafra did not bother to return his salute, but blurted instead, "Commander Djedef, I always remember your faithfulness when you saved me from certain death. I expect that you also remember my generosity to you, when you were a low-ranking soldier, and I made you into a great commander—crowning your head with everlasting glory."

"I remember this, and I do not ever forget it," Djedef declared earnestly. "It is impossible for me to forget the blessings of My Lord the Prince."

"I'm in need of your faithfulness at this moment," said the heir apparent, "to do what is ordered, and to follow my instructions without the least hesitation. Commander, do not grant leave to your army tonight. Instead, keep the soldiers where they're encamped outside the walls of Memphis. Wait for my orders, which will come to you at daybreak. Take care not to balk at carrying them out, no matter how strange they may seem. Always remember that the courageous soldier flies like an arrow toward his goal, without questioning the one who launched it."

"I hear and obey, Your Highness," said Djedef.

"Then wait at the camp for my messengers at dawn, and be careful not to forget my instructions."

The prince said this, then stood up to signal that the meeting was finished. Djedef bowed to His Highness and left the room—astounded, distracted, and confused by his bizarre command. "Why," he said to himself, "did the prince order me to keep the army in its encampment? What could these strange commands possibly be that the messengers will bring to me at dawn? What kind of enemy threatens the nation? What sort of insurrection menaces her security? Every Egyptian goes about his business peacefully under the protection of Pharaoh and his government. So why does he need the army?"

Nervously he returned to his chariot and took off in it, the lady with him. But the closer the vehicle came to Bisharu's house, the lighter seemed his uncertainty as his inner whisperings fled and his mind turned toward his family who had been awaiting him so long with great expectation. Reaching the house, he showed the lady to the guest room, then went up to be with the dearly loved people whom he also had so much longed to see.

His mother Zaya met him with open arms. She rained kisses upon him as she pressed him to her breast with fervor, not letting him go until Bisharu pried him loose from her grip, saying, "Welcome, O conquering scion! The courageous commander!"

He kissed him on the cheeks and forehead, then his brothers, Kheny and Nafa, embraced him, as well. He greeted Nafa's wife, who was carrying a nursing baby boy in her arms. She presented him to Djedef, saying, "Look at your namesake, Little Djedef! I gave him your name so that perhaps the gods will grant him glory, like his mighty uncle!"

Djedef looked at Nafa as he held the little one in his arms, then kissed his baby-soft lips, saying to his brother, "What a beautiful portrait he'd make!"

Nafa smiled—his son made him happy the same way his art did—and he took him in his arms. At that moment, Djedef found the opportunity to announce the great news of his engagement. "You won't be the only father, Nafa!"

They all awoke to what he had said, as Nafa called out with joy, "Have you chosen your partner, Commander?"

Djedef lowered his head. "Yes," he said.

His mother stared at him with ecstatic eyes. "Is it true what you say, my son?"

Quietly he answered, "Yes, my mother."

"Who is she?" she shouted.

Mana, spellbound, asked as well, "Who is she?"

"You have just come from the field of battle," laughed Nafa. "Did you woo one of the captives?"

"She is Her Highness Meresankh," he said, calmly and with pride.

"Meresankh! Pharaoh's daughter?"

"She, and none other."

Utterly astonished, they were seized by an overpowering happiness that rendered them speechless. Djedef regaled them with the story of Pharaoh's blessing upon him as tears of joy glistened in his handsome eyes. Zaya could not control herself, but burst out weeping, praying to Lord Ptah the Magnanimous, the Gracious. Bisharu was beside himself, rocking back and forth with his bloated, sagging frame. As for Nafa, he kissed the young man and laughed for a long time with glee and delight. Kheny blessed him, assuring him that the gods do not decree such glorious things without having designed some lofty purpose that no man had previously achieved. All of them kept expressing the gladness and gaiety that were uppermost in their thoughts.

Suddenly, Djedef remembered the woman that he had left in the guest room. He stood up immediately upon recalling her. Quickly relating her story, he said to his mother, "I hope that you will extend her your hospitality, Mama, until she departs our home."

"I will go down to welcome her, my son."

Djedef escorted his mother as they entered the guest room

together. "Welcome," she said. "My lady, you have arrived at your own house . . ."

The woman rose from her seat, her heavy figure drooping from the degradation and disgrace of her long captivity, and put out her hand to her generous hostess. The two women's eyes met for the first time. With lightning speed, they forgot all about their exchange of greetings as they looked at each other strangely, each as though she were struggling to pierce the heavy veil that time had pressed over the face of the distant past. At length, the eyes of the strange woman widened as she shouted with mad astonishment, "Zaya!"

Seized by panic, Zaya stared at her with intense confusion. Djedef kept looking from one to the other in bewilderment, amazed at the woman who knew his mother though she had spent twenty years of her life in the wilderness.

"How do you know my mother?" he asked her in shock.

Yet the woman paid no heed to what he said. Perhaps she hadn't even heard him—because she was entirely focused on Zaya with an absolute mania. She grew furious with her silence and screamed at her, "Zaya . . . Zaya! Aren't you Zaya? What's wrong—why don't you speak? Speak, you treacherous servant! Tell me what you did with my son! Woman, where is my son!"

Zaya said nothing, her eyes never leaving the outraged woman. But the commotion had paralyzed her; she began to shudder as her fear tore her apart, her face like that of the dead. Djedef took her by her cold hand and sat her down on the closest seat, then turned to the woman. "How did you summon the nerve to speak this way to my mother, Madam," he demanded, "after I've taken you into my house, and saved your life?"

The woman was gasping like someone about to die. What the commander who had rescued her said greatly affected her. She wanted to speak, but—besieged by emotion—she could do no more than point to his mother as if to say, "Ask her."

The young man bent down toward Zaya with compassion and asked her softly, "Mama ... do you know this woman?"

Zaya still said nothing. The woman was unable to sustain her silence as she said, her rage returning, "Ask her, 'Do you know Ruddjedet, wife of Ra?' Ask her, 'Do you remember the woman that fled with her from tyranny, twenty years ago, carrying her little child?' Speak to me, O Zaya! Tell him how you crept away under the cover of darkness, how you kidnapped my nursing son. Tell him how you abandoned me in the unknown desert, a despairing soul, facing nothing but hardship and with nothing to avail against it. That is, until the beasts found me and took me prisoner, subjecting me to torture and the humiliation of captivity for twenty long years. Speak, O Zaya. . . . Tell me, what did you do with my child? Speak!"

More and more confused, Djedef whispered in his mother's ear in torment, "Mother ... allow me, who has caused you this agony, I who brought this woman that grief has deprived of her reason ... allow me, Mama ... I will throw her out."

But she gripped his hand to prevent him from acting, and he asked her pleadingly, "Why don't you speak, Mama?"

Zaya groaned painfully, and then spoke for the first time since the stupefaction had overwhelmed her, "There's no use ... my life is finished."

The youth called out, his voice roaring like a lion, "Mother, don't say this. You have me, O Mother!"

She sighed from her ordeal. "Oh, dear Djedef, by God, I committed no evil deed, nor used evil means, but Fate has determined what was beyond a person's power to prevent. O Lord! How can my life be destroyed in a single stroke?"

The youth was nearly insane with pain. "Mama!" he cried. "Do not forget that I am at your side, defending you from all harm. What is hurting you? What causes you such grief? Whatever your past enfolds of good or of ill, it's all the same to me. There's nothing important for me to know except that you're my mother, and I'm your son that protects you—be you oppressor or oppressed, malicious or benign. I beg you not to weep when I'm beside you."

"It's impossible for you to help me!"

"Sheer nonsense, Mama! What calamity is this?"

"You will not be able to help me, dear Djedef. My God! How I built upon hopes, but I set them on the edge of a crumbling cliff! How they were almost steady and upright, then they crashed down to the lowest ground, leaving my heart a ruin in which the ravens are screeching!"

At this, the young man's emotions grew even stronger, and he turned again toward the woman—but she did not relent. Instead, she went on pressing Zaya, "Tell me, where is my son? Where is my son?"

Zaya remained speechless for a little while, then she stood up nervously and shouted at the woman, "Do you think that I betrayed you, O Ruddjedet? No—I've never betrayed anyone. I stayed awake over you on that fateful night, but the Bedouin attacked us, and I had no choice but to flee. I took pity on your baby from their evil, and carried him in my arms, racing across the desert like a madwoman. I had to run away, seeing the nature of the threat, while your falling into their hands was decreed by Fate. Afterward, I took care of your son, and devoted my life to him. My love was good for him, for he grew up to be a man honored by the world. There he is then, standing right in front of you. Have you ever seen a mortal like him before?"

Ruddjedet turned toward her son. She wanted to speak, but her tongue would not obey.

All she was able to do was to open her arms, and, hastening to him, to entwine them around his neck while her lips trembled with these words, "My son . . . my son." The young man was dumbfounded, as though he was watching a strange dream unfold. He remained silent, sometimes looking at Zaya's cadaverlike face, and sometimes at the woman hanging onto him, kissing him with a motherly fervor and clutching him to her beating breast. Zaya saw his surrender, noting in his eye a look of affection and compassion. Groaning in despair, she turned her back to them, bolting out of the room like a butchered hen.

Djedef started to move, but the woman strengthened her grip and implored him, "My son . . . my son . . . would you abandon your mother?"

The youth froze where he was, casting a long look into her face. He saw the visage that had moved his heart from the very first glance. He saw in it this time even greater purity, beauty, and misery than he had noticed before. Giving himself over in sympathy to her, he leaned his head toward her unthinkingly until he felt her lips press on his cheek. The woman sighed in relief as her eyes drowned in tears—then she began weeping, and he set about trying to ease her distress. He sat her down on the divan, taking a seat next to her as she held back her sobs, while she remained in a state between confusion and happiness over this new love in her life.

Looking at him, the woman said, "Say to me, 'Mother!'"

"Mother . . ." he said, weakly.

Then he said in bewilderment, "But I hardly understand anything . . ."

"You will learn everything, my son."

And so she recited to him all the long tale, telling him about his birth and the momentous prophecies surrounding it, and of the prodigious events that befell her—until the fortunate hour when her spirit returned to her breast at the sight of him—alive, happy, and full of glory.

3 2

The Fates guided Bisharu to hear Ruddjedet's tale without his intending it. Wanting to welcome Djedef's guest himself, he went down to greet her, arriving by chance just as Zaya was leaving like one possessed by madness. Shocked and confused, he approached the room's door with caution, behind which he heard the voice of Ruddjedet—which she had forgotten to lower—erupting as she spoke in a state of high excitement. Secretly he listened, along with Djedef, to the woman's story—from its beginning through to its end.

Afterward, he rushed from his hiding place straight to his bedroom, heedless of all things around him, his face furrowed by a seriousness reserved for the most grievous disasters. He couldn't bear to sit down, so he kept pacing back and forth, his consciousness scattered, his soul upset, his thoughts rash and reckless. He was considering what he had heard as its jumble kept running through his head, turning it up and down on its various sides, until the feverish contemplation burnt up his mind, making it like a piece of molten bronze.

Aloud he said to himself, as though addressing a stranger, "Bisharu! Oh, you wretched old man! The gods have tested you with a difficult trial."

And what a trial!

Dear, handsome Djedef, whom he had held as a suckling baby, rescued from hunger and want, and raised in the mer-

ciful eye of fatherhood—as a crawling infant, as a running
boy, and as a wholesome young man. He to whom he gave
the upbringing of a nobleman's son, and for whom he
smoothed the road to success, until he became a man worth
a nation full of men. He to whom he granted a father's affection, and his heart entire—and from whom he received the
love of a son, and filial piety, as well. Dear, beautiful Djedef,
the Fates have shown him the truth about himself—and suddenly his enemy is Pharaoh! Suddenly, he was the means
that the Lord Ra had held in store to convulse the unshakeable throne by challenging its majestic sire, and to usurp the
right of the noble heir apparent!

The Inspector of Pharaoh's Pyramid cried out again as he
spoke to himself, "Bisharu! You miserable old man! The
deities have tested you with a difficult trial!" The man's anxiety escalated and weighed more heavily upon him, as he
continued blabbering to himself in sorrow and pain.

"O beloved Djedef, whether you're the son of the martyred worker, or the heir to the priest of Ra the Most Powerful, I truly love you the way I do Kheny and Nafa—and
you have known no father but me.

"Hence, I granted you my name, out of love and compassion. By God, you are a youth whose goodness and purity
radiates from his nature like the rays of the sun. Yet, and
more's the pity, the deities made you the trustee of the greatest treason that history has ever known—treason against the
lord of the immutable throne. Betrayer of the trust of Khufu,
our mighty sire; Khufu, whose name we teach our children
to praise before they have learned how to write the sacred
script. O you Fates! Why do you delight in our torment?
Why do you throw us into tribulations and woes in the
midst of our good fortune? How would it have harmed you
if I ended my life as it began—happy, healthy, and content?"

His state of mind deteriorated as he felt his end grow
near, so he took small steps to the mirror and looked at his

sad, miserable face. Lecturing his image, he said, "Bisharu! O man who has never harmed anyone in his life! Shall dear Djedef become the first victim whom you will reach out your hand to hurt? How bizarre! Why all this torture? Why not just keep your mouth shut as though you had heard nothing? My God! The reply is preordained—that your heart would not be at ease because it belongs to Bisharu, Inspector of the Pyramid, servant of the king. Bisharu, who adores his duty excessively; Bisharu, who worships his duty like a slave. Here is the malady: you believe in duty. Truly, you have done injury to no one, yet neither have you ever relinquished your duty. Now, which of the two do you think will be first to be sold? Duty, or the avoidance of doing harm? A pupil in the primary school at Memphis could answer this question immediately. Bisharu will not end his life with an act of treachery. No, he will never sell out his sire: Pharaoh is first—Djedef comes second." He sighed in agony and grief, his soul pierced with a poisoned dagger.

He left the room with heavy steps and went down to the house's garden. On his way, as he passed the guest room, he saw Djedef standing at its door, looking deeply absorbed in thought. Bisharu's heart pounded queerly at the sight of him, and everything within and without him—his soul, breast, even his eyelids—quivered. He avoided his eyes, for fear that any conversation would reveal the tumult in his heart.

The youth glanced peculiarly at his robes of office, asking him in a weak voice, "Where are you going now . . . Father?"

Hurrying on his way, Bisharu replied, "To perform a duty that cannot be delayed, my son."

Then he mounted his wagon, telling the driver, "To Pharaoh's palace."

While the wagon was starting on its way, the armies of night were gathering on the horizon to sweep down upon the defenseless, dying day. Bisharu regarded the approaching sundown with dejected eyes, and a heart that had turned dark like the creep of evening.

"I knew that duty was both a hardship and a delight," he said to himself as he groaned with regret and chagrin. "Yet here I am swallowing only the bitter of it—not the sweet— like a fast-killing poison."

3 3

Weeping continuously, Ruddjedet told her devastating story as Djedef sat listening to her quavering voice, feeling her warm breath on his face. He gazed for a long time into her dear, tearful eyes, ripped nearly to pieces by sorrow, pity, and pain.

When her tragic tale was done, she asked him, "Who, my son, is the priest of Ra?"

"Shudara!" he replied.

"I'm so sorry that your father was made a victim—through no fault of his own."

"This surprise has me utterly confused. . . . Only yesterday I was Djedef son of Bisharu, while today I'm a new person, whose past is full of calamities. Born to a father who was killed at the time, and a wretched mother suffering the life of a prisoner for all of twenty years. How fantastic! My birth was accursed—I'm so sorry for that, Mother!"

"Don't say that, my dear son, and burden your pure soul with the sin of the Accursed Satan."

"How horrible! My father was killed, and you endured torment for twenty long years!"

"May the gods have mercy on my son," she abjured. "Forget your sorrows and think about how things will end—my heart is not reassured."

"What do you mean, Mama?"

"Danger still surrounds us, O my son. It menaces you today through him who provided for you yesterday."

"How incredible! Could I, Djedef, be an enemy of Pharaoh? And Pharaoh—who bestowed upon me all his blessings every day, and generously granted me his favors—is he the slayer of my father and the torturer of my mother?"

"No one can keep silent who watches people and the world. So look toward the end, because I don't want to lose you on the very day that I found you, after the torment of the years."

"Where should we go, Mama?"

"The Lord's land is wide."

"How can I flee like a felon when I have committed no crime?"

"Had your father done anything wrong?"

"My nature scorns flight," he replied.

"Take pity on my heart, which is torn to bits by fear."

"Do not fear, Mother," he consoled her. "My devotion and loyalty to the throne will serve on my behalf with Pharaoh."

"Nothing will serve on your behalf with him for anything," she admonished, "when he discovers that you are his rival, whom the gods created to inherit his throne."

The youth's eyes widened in disbelief. "Inherit his throne?" he cried. "How misguided a prophecy is this!"

"I beg you, my son, to put my heart at rest."

He took her in his arms, pressing against her with compassion. "I have lived twenty years, without anyone knowing my secret," he said. "Forgetfulness has enfolded it—and it shall not arise again."

"I know not, Son, why I am frightened and apprehensive. Perhaps it is Zaya. . . ."

"Zaya!" he exclaimed. "For all of twenty long years I called her my mother. If motherhood were mercy, love, and personal devotion, then she was my mother, too, Mama. Zaya would never wish evil upon us. She is an ill-fated woman, like a virtuous queen who has lost her throne without warning."

But before Ruddjedet could open her mouth to respond, a male servant entered hurriedly, saying that Djedef's deputy Sennefer wanted to meet him immediately, without the slightest delay. The young man was taken aback, because Sennefer had been with him only a short time before. He reassured his fearful mother as he excused himself to go out to meet Sennefer in the garden. Djedef found the officer anxious, impatient, and upset. The moment Sennefer saw him he came up to him quickly, without any greetings or graces.

"Commander, sir," he burst out, "by chance I have learned of sinister facts that warn of an impending evil!"

Djedef's heart raced, and he turned and looked unconsciously back at the guest room as he wondered to himself, "Do you see what new adversities the Fates have hidden from you?"

Then he looked at his deputy. "What do you mean by that, Sennefer?"

In bewildered accents, the officer told him: "Just before sunset today, I went into the wine cellar to pick out a good bottle. I was looking about waywardly—standing next to the skylight that looks out onto the garden—when I heard the voice of the crown prince's chief chamberlain talking in whispers with a strange person. Though I couldn't make out what they were saying clearly, I did hear him well when he finished by calling him, 'Prince Khafra, who will be Pharaoh by dawn tomorrow!' I was jolted by terror, as I was sure that His Majesty the King must have gone to be near Osiris. I forgot what I had been looking for and hurried outside to the soldiers' barracks. I found the officers playing around and chatting as they usually do when off-duty, so I thought that the dreadful news had not yet reached them. I didn't want to be the bearer of evil tidings, so I slipped away outside, mounted my chariot and headed toward Pharaoh's palace, where I might establish the truth of the matter. I saw that the palace was quiet, its lights twinkling as always like brilliant stars, the guards going to and fro with no sign of anything wrong. Undoubtedly, it seemed, the lord of the palace was alive and well. I was stunned at what I'd heard in the cellar, and thought about it for a long time. I was worried and afraid. Then your person came to my mind, like a light leading a ship lost in the dark, at the mercy of the wind and waves in a violent storm, safely into shore. So I came to you urgently, hoping to take your wise direction."

Agitated, Djedef asked him—having forgotten his personal troubles, and all that had taken him so much by surprise that day, "Are you sure that your ears did not deceive you?"

"My presence before you now is proof that I'm sure."

"You aren't drunk?"

"I haven't tasted drink this day at all."

The young commander fixed him with a frozen stare, and asked in what he imagined was a strange voice indeed, "And what did you understand from this?"

The officer fell fearfully silent, as though guarding his answer, leaving the commander to supply it himself. Djedef understood what lay behind his failure to speak, his heart pounding as he became lost in thought. At that moment, he remembered Prince Khafra's peculiar instructions: his order not to discharge his soldiers, and to await his commands at dawn—and to follow them, however unusual they might seem. These disquieting memories returned as he thought of what Sennefer, who stood before him now, had told him—on his first day as a guard to the prince—about the heir apparent's character, his short temper, and his severity. He recalled all of this quickly and with shock, as he wondered, "What else are you holding back, O World of the Invisible? Is Pharaoh in danger? Is there treason abroad in Egypt?"

He heard Sennefer say with passion, "We are soldiers of Khafra, but we swore our oath of loyalty to the king. The army altogether is Pharaoh's men—except for the traitors."

He realized that Sennefer's suspicions matched his own. "I fear that the king is in peril!" he said, heatedly.

"I've no doubt of that—we must do something, O Commander," said Sennefer.

"Most nights, the king spends inside his pyramid with his vizier Hemiunu, dictating his great book-in-progress," said Djedef. "We must take our warning to the pyramid—I'm afraid that the treachery will be enacted against him while he's there in the burial chamber."

"That's not possible," Sennefer replied. "Only three persons know the secret of how to open the pyramid's door—the king, Hemiunu, and Mirabu. And the plateau encircling the pyramid is full of guards, both day and night, plus priests of the god Osiris."

In an afterthought, Sennefer asked, "Does one of the king's guards ride with him in his chariot?"

"No, the great monarch who has devoted his life to Egypt does not feel the need for protection among his subjects, in his own country. I believe, O Sennefer—if our suspicions are correct—that the danger is crouching, ready to pounce, in the Valley of Death. That is a long road, devoid of any people, whose solitude would tempt the traitor to ambush his prey."

Gasping, Sennefer asked, "What should we do?"

"Our mission is twofold," Djedef told him. "That we warn the king of the danger, and that we arrest the traitors."

"What if there are princes among them?"

"Even if the crown prince himself is among them!"

"My dear commander, we should not rely upon the heir apparent's guards."

"You have spoken wisely, Sennefer," Djedef replied. "We've no need of them—for we have a courageous army, every soldier of which would not hesitate to sacrifice his life for the sake of our sire."

Sennefer's face lit up as he said, "So let's summon the army right away!"

But the young commander placed his hand on his zealous deputy's shoulder. "The army should not be called upon except to fight another army like itself," he said. "Our enemy—if our concerns are real—is a tiny band that seeks refuge in darkness, plotting their evil by night. Let's lie in wait for them and hit them the decisive blow before they aim their blow at us."

"But, Commander, sir, hadn't we better warn Pharaoh?"

"That's bad counsel, Sennefer," cautioned Djedef. "We have no proof of this appalling treason except our own doubts—and they could be mere illusions. Hence, we can't warn Pharaoh yet about our dangerous accusation against his own crown prince!"

"So then, what should we do, Commander, sir?"

"The wise thing would be for me to choose several tens of officers of those whose courage I am confident—and you'll be among them, Sennefer," the youth said. "Then, one by one, we'll hide in the Valley of Death. We'll spread ourselves throughout all its sides, alert, vigilant, and in wait. We'd better not waste time—we must beat our enemy to his ambush, so that we see him before he sees us."

To be sure, the young man did not waste a moment. Yet, despite the vital importance of what he had to do, he could not forget his mother. He took her to Nafa's wing of their house, putting her in care of Nafa's wife, Mana. Then he returned to Sennefer, riding with him in his chariot to the military encampment outside the walls of Memphis. Along the way, he spoke to himself.

"Now I understand why the prince commanded me to await his orders at dawn, for he has a gambit planned to kill his father," he thought. "In the event that he accomplished this goal, he wanted me to stealthily march the army on the capital in order to finish off the Great House Guards, along with the king's faithful men such as Hemiunu, Mirabu, Arbu, and the others from Pharaoh's inner circle. Thus he would clear the field to announce his impatient self as king over Egypt. What despicable treachery!"

"No doubt, the prince feels he can wait no longer," he went on addressing himself. "But his own ambitions will condemn his hopes when they are only two bow lengths or less from reaching fruition. But will our suspicions turn out to be true—or are we beating our heads against mere errors and delusions?"

Dawn appeared, and life began yet again on the sacred pyramid plateau, as the shouts of the guards, the blasts of the horns, and the chanting of the priests echoed in the sky overhead. Amidst all this, the pyramid's door opened and two specters emerged from within, before it was closed and sealed once again. Each of these figures was wrapped in a thick cloak resembling those worn by priests during the feasts of sacrifice. The shorter of the two said to the other, "My lord, you're exerting your sublime self quite unsparingly."

"It seems, Hemiunu," answered the king, "that the further we progress in age, the more we return to our childhood. How my ardor for this majestic labor resembles my former passion for the chase and for riding horses! Indeed, I must redouble my efforts, Hemiunu—for what remains of my life now is but the briefest part."

The vizier, who had also been made a prince, stretched out his hands in prayer. "May the gods lengthen the life of the king," he intoned.

"May the gods answer your prayer until I have finished my book," said Khufu.

"I would never forbid the doing of good," replied Hemiunu, "but I do wish that our lord be given eternal peace and comfort."

"No, O Hemiunu," said the king. "Egypt has built me a

204 / Naguib Mahfouz

place of rest for my soul, while I grant her nothing but my own mortal life."

The two men stopped talking as Khufu mounted the royal chariot. Then the vizier clambered in and grasped the reins, as the horses moved in an ambling gate. Each time that the vehicle passed a group of soldiers or priests, they prostrated themselves in salute and respect. The horses trotted steadily until they traversed the plateau and crossed its borders to the Valley of Death, which led to the gates of Memphis. The darkness was still pitch-black and the sky filled with stars, twinkling so intensely that it might make an observer think that they were falling upon another nearby, bewitching hearts with their encompassing majesty.

Midway through the Valley of Immortality, as the king and his chief minister rode in quiet meditation, they were startled to hear one of their steeds scream violently, before leaping in the air and falling to the ground. The horse's collapse prevented the chariot from continuing, and stopped the second stallion in his tracks. The two men were amazed, and the vizier thought of going down to see what had felled the lead horse. But before he could move, he shrieked in pain and shouted, "Take care, sire—I am wounded!"

Khufu grasped that a human being had struck the horse before targeting the vizier, as well. Thinking this must be a highway robber, he called out powerfully, "Flee, you coward! Who is it that would assassinate Pharaoh?"

But then he heard a voice like thunder yell, "To me, Sennefer!" Looking at the place whence it came—as he clutched the stricken Hemiunu to his breast—he saw a ghost coming out from the right side of the valley like an arrow in flight. Next, the voice boomed out again, "Shield yourself within your chariot, my lord!"

Meanwhile he saw standing on the road, another ghost, which had come from the left side of the valley. The two shades fought each other viciously, trading murderous blows with their swords. Then one of them screeched and crashed to the ground—dead, without a doubt. But which of them had fallen, the friend or the foe? Yet the king's anxiety did not last long, for he heard the voice of his savior ask, "Is my lord alright?"

"Yes, O valiant one," he answered. "But my vizier is hurt."

Just then, Khufu heard the clash of blades behind his chariot. Turning quickly, he saw a detachment of troops embroiled in seething combat, and the courageous man who had slain his would-be assassin join them, as troop vanquished troop. The king watched the battle in hapless anger.

The fighting tipped in favor of Pharaoh's supporters as they brought down their adversaries one by one. Terror gripped the traitors as, in the distance, they spotted a squadron of horsemen approaching from the direction of the holy plateau, bearing torches and cheering the name of their glorious king. Rattled with fright, they sought to escape—but those who opposed them were stronger and more ruthless. They cut them off and killed them, sparing not one.

The arriving knights encircled Pharaoh's chariot, their torches lighting up the valley to reveal the corpses of the enemy dead. The faces of those who fell defending the king were also exposed, their blameless blood streaming down over their necks and their brows.

The horsemen's chief advanced upon Khufu's vehicle—and when he saw his sire standing upright, he praised the god as he knelt in reverence. "How is Our Lord the King?" he asked.

Khufu held up his vizier as he came down from his chariot. "Pharaoh is well, thanks to the gods, and to the valor of these men," he said.

"But how are you, Hemiunu?"

"I'm fine, my lord," he answered weakly. "I was hit in the forearm, but that's not fatal by itself. Let's all pray in thanks to Ptah, who saved our king's life."

Pharaoh peered around him and saw the young commander. "You're here, Commander Djedef? Are you trying to put all of the royal family together in your debt!" he exclaimed.

The youth bowed in deep respect. "We all—each one of us—would sacrifice ourselves for our lord," he replied.

"But how did this happen?" asked the king. "To me it appears that what occurred here was no trifling event, certainly not coincidence. I could just perceive in the dark a case of high treason, foiled by your loyalty and your bravery. But first we must have a look at the faces of those killed. Let's begin with the one who rashly fired arrows at us, to halt us on our way. . . ."

Djedef, Sennefer, and the head of the horsemen marched with the torches before the king in the direction of the chariot, Hemiunu following him with ponderous steps. They came upon someone after only a short distance, sprawled on his face, the fatal shaft buried in his left side, groaning in pain. The king started at the sound, and—hurrying to him—he turned him on his back. Casting a worried glance upon him, when he saw his face he howled aloud, "Khafra . . . my son!"

All majesty forgotten, Khufu stared at those around him as though appealing for their aid against this tribulation that seemed irresistible. He studied the face of the man lying at his feet once more, and said in grief and revulsion, "Are you the one who attempted to slay me?"

But the prince was in the throes of his final agony, slipping into the unconsciousness of one who is leaving this world. He paid no heed to the horrified eyes now fixed upon him, but continued to moan plaintively, his chest heaving violently. A stifling quiet descended over all of them, in which Hemiunu forgot his aching arm, but kept stealing furtive looks of pity at Khufu's face, who was imploring the Lord to spare him the evil of that moment. Pharaoh leaned over his expiring son, regarding him with hardened eyes that trauma made look like two stagnant pools. His soul was dazed and disturbed, conflicting thoughts and emotions clashing within him, as he surrendered to indifference. He went on gaping at the agonizing crown prince until the final glint of glory abandoned him, and his body ceased moving for all eternity.

The king remained frozen in his queer immobility for not a short while. Then his own majesty and confidence returned as he stood up straight. Turning to Djedef, he asked in an unfamiliar voice, "Inform me, O Commander, of all the details that you know about this matter."

In a voice shuddering with sorrow, Djedef told his sire of what the officer Sennefer had reported to him, of the doubts that assailed them, and of the ruse that they devised to rescue their lord.

"By the gods!" cried Khufu.

He had been going and coming without any concern, only to be caught unawares by infamy from where he had not at all expected it—from his most precious son, his own heir apparent. The gods had saved him from the terrible evil, but in carrying out their will, they had cost him very dear. This was the spirit that now went up, polluted with the most repugnant sin that a mortal can commit. Pharaoh had survived annihilation, but he felt no delight. His crown prince had been killed, and he did not know how to grieve for him. The world had shown him its most despicable face, just as he was reaching the end of his path.

The king and his companions returned to the royal palace that morning, as the world was adorned with the rising sun. The all-powerful monarch felt a spiritless fatigue, so he made his way quickly to his chamber and collapsed onto his bed. The awful news spread through the vastness of the palace, carrying with it sadness and dismay. Queen Meritites was shaken to her foundations, a consuming fire exploding within her, of which not all the waters of the Nile could extinguish a single brand. The woman stuck close to her great husband seeking to ward off the woe of this evil by her nearness to him, as well as to obtain his reassurance and consolation. She found him sleeping, or like one asleep, and touched his forehead with her chill fingers to discover that he was as hot as a mass of fire, sending up embers into the air.

She whispered to him in a faltering voice, "My lord!"

The king stirred at the sound, opening his eyes in a state of indignant turmoil. He sat up in his bed in unaccustomed rage, piercing her with a glare that sent off sparks. In a maddened tone that had not been heard before, he demanded of his spouse, "Are you weeping, O Queen, for the damned assassin?"

"I am weeping for my miserable fortune, my sire," she answered submissively, her tears overflowing.

Insane with rage, he bellowed, "Woman, you bore me a criminal for a son!"

"My lord!"

"The divine wisdom decreed his death because the throne was not created to be occupied by criminals!"

"Mercy, my lord!" the woman wailed. "Mercy for my heart, and for yours! Don't speak to me in this terrifying tone—I need consoling. Let's forget this agonizing memory: he was our son, and now he deserves mourning!"

He shook his head with lunatic fury. "I see that you are showing him mercy!"

"We're entitled to weep, sire. Didn't he lose both this world and the hereafter?"

Khufu grabbed his head and raved in confusion, "My God . . . what is this madness that runs through my mind! What are these blows that keep falling on Pharaoh's head? How can it bear the crown of the Egyptians after this moment, when it is weighed down just by the white hairs that time has left on it? O Queen, Pharaoh is suffering a new phase of life, and all of your own suffering will be of no avail. So call for my sons and daughters, and all of my friends. Summon Hemiunu, Mirabu, Arbu, and Djedef—go on, then!"

The wretched queen left the king's chamber, and sent out a request for the princes, the princesses, and their father's companions. On her own, she also asked for Kara, the king's private physician.

Each of them answered the call, coming promptly and in speechless shock, as though they were heading for a dreadful wake. They entered Pharaoh's room. He did not tarry on his bed but walked between the two lines of them, that of his immediate family, and the second of his other relatives and friends. The king was still vilely upset, his gaze wandering, when he caught sight of Kara, interrogating him gruffly. "Why did you come here, Doctor, without my asking for you?" he demanded. "You have been with me for all of forty years, and I have never once needed you in all that time.

Should not one who can dispense with his doctor in his lifetime, be able to do the same when he dies?"

Mention of death frightened them, for its effect on Pharaoh's nerves and his state of uproar. As for the physician Kara, he smiled delicately, saying, "My lord is in need of a draught of . . ."

Khufu cut him off, shouting, "Take leave of your lord, and vanish from my sight!"

The sadness was plain on Kara's face as he said quietly, "My lord, perhaps—at times—the physician must disobey an order from his sire."

The king's rage grew greater as he shifted his straying eyes through the faces of those arrayed, dumbfounded, around him, then bellowed, "Don't you hear what this man is saying? And you all stand there doing nothing about it? How extraordinary! Has treason infected every heart here? Is Pharaoh despised by all of his children, and his friends? O Vizier Hemiunu—tell me what's fitting to do with one who defies Pharaoh!"

Hemiunu came forth with obvious weariness and whispered in the doctor's ear. The man bowed to his lord and retreated to the background before exiting the chamber.

Meanwhile, Hemiunu drew close to Khufu's bed. "Go easy, sire, for what did the man want to do but good? Would my lord like me to fetch him a cup of water?"

Without awaiting the king's permission, the vizier left the room and Kara gave him a golden goblet filled with water in which a sedative potion had been stirred. The minister carried it to Khufu, who took it from Hemiunu's hand and drank it to the last drop. Swiftly feeling its effects, the king's agitation subsided as his normal expression returned, his flushed face regaining its natural color. Yet his frailty and listlessness were clear to see, as well.

Sighing deeply, the king said, "Woe to the person who

suffers from old age and feebleness. These two weaklings shake the strongest giants!"

He looked at the group gathered around his bed. "I was a ruler of overwhelming vigor!" he lamented. "I was famed for my right hand, which clove between life and death! I pronounced laws both sacred and profane, inspiring worship and obedience! In my life, never for a moment did I forget my plan of good works and reform. I did not want the benefit for my servants to end with my life on earth. Hence, I wrote a lengthy thesis on medicine and wisdom which will be useful for as long as diseases show no mercy to the human being, and so long as the human being shows no mercy to himself. My life was prolonged, as you all see, and the gods wanted to test me with a severe trial of whose wisdom I was ignorant. They chose my son as their instrument and unleashed the armies of evil in his heart. He rose up as my enemy by ambushing me in the dark in order to kill me. Yet, my survival was written, and the ill-fated son paid the price of his life—for the sake of the few hours left in my own."

The group listening called out wishfully, "May God lengthen the king's life!"

Pharaoh raised his hand, and silence returned before he resumed his address. "The end is decreed," he declared. "I've summoned you to hear my last speech. Are you all prepared?"

Hemiunu was awash with tears. "My lord! Do not mention Death. . . . This sorrow will be lifted—and you'll live long, for Egypt, and for us."

Pharaoh smiled. "Grieve not, O friend Hemiunu," he admonished. "If Death were an evil, then immortality would have kept Mina on the throne of Egypt. Therefore, Khufu does not sorrow over death, nor does he dread it. Death is a less critical injury than many others that deform the face of life. Yet I want to be at ease concerning my grand bequest."

He turned toward his sons, examining each of them one by one, as though he were trying to read what lay behind and inside them.

"I see you holding back in silence," he said, "anxiously concealing a hidden sorrow. Each one of you regards his brother with a suspicious and resentful eye. And how could this not be so, when the heir apparent has died? The king is dying, and each of you harbors ambitions toward the throne, wanting it for himself. I do not deny that you are all noble youths of lofty morals—but I want to put myself at rest about my succession, and about your brethren."

Baufra, the oldest of the princes, interrupted him. "My father and my lord," he said, "however our longings may have divided us, they have conditioned us to obey you. Your will for us is like the holy law that compels our subservience without any dissent."

The king grinned ruefully, beholding them with eyes that swiveled exhaustedly in their sockets. "What you said is beautiful, O Baufra," he said. "Truly, I say to you, that I, at this frightful hour, find within myself an overawing power over the sublimity of human emotions. I feel that my fatherhood over the believers is of more import than my fatherhood toward my sons. They have appointed me to say what is right—and to do it, as well."

Once again, he scrutinized their expressions, then proceeded, "To me, it seems that what I have said now has caused you no astonishment. And the truth is that, without disavowing my fatherhood of you, I find before me one who is more deserving of the throne than any of you, one whose assuming the crown will help preserve the virtue of your own brothers. He is a youth whose zeal has long destined him for leadership, while his courage has achieved a magnificent victory for the homeland. His heroism saved Pharaoh's life from perfidy. Be sure not to ask, 'How can he sit on Egypt's throne if the blood of kings flows not in his veins?' For he is the husband of Princess Meresankh, in whose veins runs the blood of kings and queens alike."

Djedef looked astounded as he exchanged confused glances with Meresankh, while the princes and men of state were all caught so off-guard that their tongues were frozen and their eyes seemed dazed. They all stared at Djedef.

Prince Baufra was the first to risk rupturing this silence. "My lord, saving the king's life is a duty for every person, and not the sort of deed that anyone would hesitate to perform. Therefore, how can the throne be his reward?"

Sternly, the king replied, "I see that you would now stoke the fires of rebellion after having sung the anthems of obedience but a short while ago. O my sons, you are the princes of the realm and its lords. You shall have wealth, influence, and position—but the throne shall be Djedef's. This is the last will of Khufu, which he proclaims to his sons, by the right he has over them to command their obedience. Let the vizier hear it, so that he may carry it out by his authority and by his word. Let the supreme commander hear it also, that he may guard its execution with the force of his army. This last bequest of Khufu he leaves in the presence of those that he loves, and who love him; of those with whom he has dwelt closely in amity, and who, in return, offer their affection and fidelity."

An intimidating silence settled over them, that none dared to disturb, as each withdrew to his own thoughts—until there entered the chief chamberlain. He prostrated himself before the king, then announced, "My lord, the Inspector of the Pyramid, Bisharu, begs Your Majesty for an audience with you."

"Invite him to come in, for from this moment he belongs to our household."

Bisharu entered with his short height and wide girth, and prostrated himself before Pharaoh. Afterward, the king ordered him to stand, granting him permission to speak.

His voice subdued, the man said, "Sire! I wanted to appear before Your Majesty last night about something very important, but I arrived just after my lord's departure for the pyramid. Hence I had to wait, with much apprehension, until this morning."

"What do you wish to say, O father of brave Djedef?"

"My lord," Bisharu continued, his voice even lower, as he stared at the floor, "I am not the father of Djedef, and Djedef is not my son."

Stunned, Pharaoh replied with mocking irony, "Yesterday, a son denies his father—and today, a father denies his son!"

In sorrow, Bisharu went on, "My lord, all of the gods know that I love this young man with the affection of a father for his son. I wouldn't say these words if my loyalty to the throne were not greater in me than the sway of human emotions."

The king's perplexity multiplied, as the interest grew in the faces of all those in attendance—especially the princes, who hoped that a disaster for the young man would rescue them from the king's final testament. They all kept glancing back and forth between Bisharu and Djedef, whose color had gone pale, his expression rigid.

"What do you mean by this, Inspector?" Pharaoh asked the disavowing father.

Still staring at the floor, Bisharu answered, "Sire . . . Djedef is the son of the former priest of Ra, whose name was Monra."

Pharaoh fixed him with an odd, dreamlike look, as ambition stirred among all those listening discreetly, while the eyes of Hemiunu, Mirabu, and Arbu seemed disturbed. Khufu, however, muttered in confusion while his spirit floated through the darkness of the distant past, saying to himself, "Ra! Monra, the Priest of Ra!"

The architect Mirabu's memory was most vivid of that traumatic day that had carved its events into his consciousness. "The son of Monra?" he said with disbelief. "That is far from being credible, my lord—for Ra died, and his son was killed, in the same instant."

Pharaoh's memory returned in an aureole of fire. His tired, weakened heart convulsed as he spoke.

"Yes—the son of Monra was massacred on the bed where he was born. What do you say to this, Bisharu?"

"Sire," replied the inspector, "I have no knowledge of the child that was slaughtered. All that I know of this ancient history came to me by chance, or through wisdom known only to the Lord. It has been a trial for my heart that is attached to this lad in every possible manner, yet my fidelity to the king calls upon me to recount it."

And so Bisharu told his sovereign—as his eyes brimmed with honorable tears—the story of Zaya and her nursing baby boy, from its beginning to the appalling moment when he stood eavesdropping upon Ruddjedet's strange tale. When the man had finished his unhappy narrative, he bowed his head down to his chest, and spoke no more.

Astonishment gripped all those there, the eyes of the princes gleaming with a sudden hope. As for Princess Mere-sankh, her eyes widened with shock and awe, while her heart went mad with fear, pain, and anticipation. Her attention focused on her father's face—or on his mouth, as if she wanted to suppress, with her spirit, the words that might condemn her happiness and her expectations.

Turning his blanched face toward Djedef, the king asked him, "Is it true what this man is saying, Commander?"

With his constant courage, Djedef replied, "My lord! What Inspector Bisharu has said is true, without any doubt."

Pharaoh looked to Hemiunu, then to Arbu, and finally to Mirabu, pleading for help against the terror of these wonders. "What a marvel this is!" he exclaimed.

Glaring at Djedef, Prince Baufra declared, "Now the truth has come to light!"

Pharaoh, however, paid no heed to his son's remark, but began to recite in a fading, delirious voice: "Some twenty years ago, I proclaimed a war against the Fates, ruthlessly challenging the will of the gods. With a small army that I headed myself, I set out to do battle with a nursing child. Everything appeared to me that it would proceed according to my own desire, and I was not troubled by doubt of any kind. I thought that I had executed my own will, and raised the respect for my word. Verily, today my self-assurance is made ridiculous, and now—by the Lord—my pride is battered. Here you all see how I repaid the baby of Ra for killing my heir apparent by choosing him to succeed me on the throne of Egypt. What a marvel this is!"

Pharaoh let his head droop until his beard rested upon his breast, sinking into deep meditation. All gathered realized that the king was about to issue a judgment that he would not retract, so again they fell into a morbid stillness. The princes waited in anguish, fear and hope fighting violently inside them. Princess Meresankh gazed at her father with staring eyes, from which an angel of goodness looked out, pleading and beseeching. Tearfully they glistened with the gleam of concern as they ran back and forth between the king's head and the valiant youth that stood with enormous stoicism, capitulating to the Fates.

Prince Baufra's patience snapped. "My lord, with just one word, you could realize your decree, and make your will victorious!" he railed.

Khufu lifted up his head like one waking from a sound slumber and looked at his son for a long time. He glanced at the faces of the others present, then said calmly, "Pharaoh is good earth, like the land of his kingdom, and beneficial knowledge flourishes within it. If not for the ignorance and folly of youth, he would not have murdered innocent, blameless souls."

Once more, the silence returned, as bitter disappointment

tested many there, pierced by the poisoned dagger of despair. Princess Meresankh sighed so audibly that it reached the ears of the king—and he recognized its source. He looked at her with pity and compassion, motioning to her with his hand. She flew to him like a dove trained in flight, then bowed her head while kissing the hand that summoned her.

Looking to Hemiunu, the king said, "Bring me papyrus, O Vizier, that I may conclude my book of wisdom with the gravest lesson that I have learned in my life. And be quick— for I have only a few moments left to live."

The minister brought the folds of papyrus, and Pharaoh opened them upon his lap. He grasped the reed pen and began to write his last admonition, as Meresankh knelt next to his bed, along with the grieving queen. As all held their breath, the only sound was the scratching of the king's pen.

When Pharaoh finished writing, he threw the pen away with a potent dissipation. As he let his head drop onto the pillow, he pronounced with effort, "Khufu's message to his beloved people is now complete."

The king began to moan deeply and heavily. But before he surrendered to total rest, he looked at Djedef and signaled him to come. The youth approached Pharaoh's bed and stood still as a statue, as Khufu took his hand and placed it into the hand of Meresankh. He placed his own gaunt hand upon theirs, then looked at the people around him.

"O princes, ministers, and companions, all of you hail the monarchs of tomorrow."

Not one of them replied, as, with heads bowed, they all turned toward Djedef and Meresankh.

Khufu, motionless, stared at the room's ceiling. The queen, worried, leaned toward him a little. She found his face bathed in a celestial light, as though he saw—in his mind's eye—Mighty Osiris gazing down from on high.

Glossary

Arsina: Evidently related to the Hebrew name for Mt. Sinai (Har-Sinai, pronounced *harsina*).

Baba: The second month of the Coptic calendar, roughly corresponding to Gregorian October.

Barmuda: The eighth month of the Coptic calendar, roughly corresponding to Gregorian April.

breed of Armant: This well-known type of dog, medium-sized with a build similar to a Labrador retriever, is believed to have originated in pharaonic times from the area of Armant (ancient Iunu-Montu, later Hermonthis) in Upper Egypt. The breed's sandy coloring has given rise to a somewhat derogatory popular expression said of fair-complexioned people, *asfar zayy kalb armanti*—"blond as a dog from Armant."

Hatur and Kiyahk: These two months, roughly corresponding to Gregorian November and December, are the third and fourth Coptic months respectively.

Hemiunu: In the Arabic original, Mahfouz named the vizier "Khumini," evidently a corruption of Hemiunu, a historical figure who was actually Khufu's chief architect, minister of works, and probable designer of the Great Pyramid.

mastaba tombs: The shape of this type of burial structure, commonly used in the Predynastic Period and early Old Kingdom, resembled the mud-brick benches found in public places in Egypt, called *mastabas* in Arabic. The word itself is drawn from ancient Egyptian.

Mirabu: According to Old Kingdom specialist Rainer Stadelmann, during the reign of Khufu, a chief engineer under supreme architect Hemiunu (see above), was called Meryb. This is the probable source for the name of Khufu's master builder in this novel—whose character and role Mahfouz conflated with that of the historical Hemiunu.

Per-Usir: "Abode of Osiris," the Predynastic cult center of the underworld god, and the likely place of his cult's origin, located in the Delta at the site of the modern town of Abusir-Bana, south of Samannud. The Greek writer Strabo also called it Cynopolis.

Piramesse: Capital city of the New Kingdom (Nineteenth Dynasty) monarch, Ramesses II (r. 1304–1227 B.C.), located in the Eastern Delta at modern Qantir.

reposes next to Osiris/gone to be near Osiris: Euphemisms derived from the belief that the dead were under the authority of Osiris, chief god of the underworld.

rotl: A measure used in several Arabic-speaking, Mediterranean countries, varying from roughly one pound (as in Egypt) up to five pounds in other countries.

Tut: The first month of the Coptic calendar, named for Thoth, the ancient Egyptian god of writing and magic, and roughly corresponding to Gregorian September.

Valley of Death/Valley of Eternity: The long causeway connecting the pyramid to the king's mortuary temple, which lay in the valley to the east. Contrary to its depiction here, the causeway was not open, but walled and decorated (and in later times, covered). The Valley Temple of Khufu's pyramid was built in what is now part of the modern village of Nazlat al-Summan at the foot of the Giza Plateau. While its causeway has largely been excavated by archaeologists, the temple itself remains buried beneath modern buildings.

wall (in Sinai): In *Khufu's Wisdom*, the Bedouin renegades use a wall or other fortification for protection against the assault of the army led by Djedef in the region of Mt. Sinai. Historically, beginning perhaps late in the Old Kingdom (2687–2191 B.C.), but especially in the Middle Kingdom (2061–1664 B.C.), the Egyptians built a series of fortifications now known as the Wall of the Prince, to defend the Nile Valley from the depredations of Asiatic tribes entering the country through the Sinai Peninsula.

AKHENATEN
Dweller in Truth

The "heretic pharaoh," Akhenaten, who ruled Egypt during the 18th Dynasty (1540–1307 B.C.) was at once cruel and empathic, feminine and barbaric, mad and divinely inspired, eerily modern, and fascinatingly ethereal. In Mahfouz's novel, after the pharaoh's mysterious death, a young man questions Akhenaten's closest friends, his bitter enemies, and finally his enigmatic wife, Nefertiti, in an effort to discover what really happened in those dark days at Akhenaten's court.

Fiction/Literature/0-385-49909-4

ARABIAN NIGHTS AND DAYS

A renowned Nobel Prize–winning novelist refashions the classic tales of Scheherazade in his own imaginative, spellbinding style. Here are genies and flying carpets, Aladdin and Sinbad, Ali Baba, and many other familiar stories made new by the magical pen of the acknowledged dean of Arabic letters.

Fiction/Literature/0-385-46901-2

THE BEGGAR, THE THIEF AND THE DOGS, AUTUMN QUAIL

In *The Beggar*, a man sacrifices his work and family to a series of illicit love affairs. Released from jail in post-Revolutionary times, the hero of *The Thief and the Dogs* blames an unjust society for his ill fortune, eventually bringing himself to destruction. *Autumn Quail* is a tale of political downfall about a corrupt bureaucrat who is one of the early victims of the purge after the 1952 revolution in Egypt.

Fiction/Literature/0-385-49835-7

THE DAY THE LEADER WAS KILLED

The year is 1981, Anwar al-Sadat is president, and Egypt is lurching into the modern world. *The Day the Leader Was Killed* relates the tale of a middle-class Cairene family. Rich with irony and infused with politics, the story is narrated alternately by the pious and mischievous family patriarch Muhtashimi Zayed, his hapless grandson Elwan, and Elwan's headstrong and beautiful fiancée, Randa.

Fiction/Literature/0-385-49922-1

ECHOES OF AN AUTOBIOGRAPHY

Here, in his first work of nonfiction to be published in the United States, Mahfouz considers the myriad perplexities of existence including the preoccupation with old age and death and life's transitory nature. A departure from his bestselling and much-loved fiction, this unusual and thoughtful book is breathtaking evidence of the fact that Naguib Mahfouz is also a profound thinker of the first order.

Biography/Autobiography/0-385-48556-5

VOICES FROM THE OTHER WORLD
Ancient Egyptian Tales

From the Predynastic Period, where a cabal of entrenched rulers banish virtue in jealous defense of their status, to the Fifth Dynasty, where a Pharaoh returns from an extended leave to find that only his dog has remained loyal, to the twentieth century, where a mummy from the Eighteenth Dynasty awakens in fury to reproach a modern Egyptian nobleman for his arrogance, these five stories bring the world of ancient Egypt face-to-face with our own times.

Fiction/Literature/Short Stories/1-4000-7666-8

ALSO AVAILABLE:
Adrift on the Nile, 0-385-42333-0
The Beginning and the End, 0-385-26458-5
Children of the Alley, 0-385-26473-9
The Harafish, 0-385-42335-7
The Journey of Ibn Fattouma, 0-385-42334-9
Midaq Alley, 0-385-26476-3
Miramar, 0-385-26478-X
Palace of Desire, 0-385-26468-2
Palace Walk, 0-385-26466-6
Respected Sir, Wedding Song, The Search, 0-385-49836-5
Sugar Street, 0-385-26470-4
The Time and the Place, 0-385-26472-0

ⓣ
ANCHOR BOOKS
Available at your local bookstore, or call toll-free to order:
1-800-793-2665 (credit cards only).